MY NAME IS AMERICA

The Journal of Finn Reardon

A Newsie

BY SUSAN CAMPBELL BARTOLETTI

Scholastic Inc. New York

New York City
1899

Sunday, January 1, 1899

Today is the first day of the New Year. It feels strange writing 1899 at the top of this page, but it will feel even stranger writing 1900 next year.

Ma gave me this new journal for Christmas, and I suppose that now is as good a time as any to write in it. I got my first journal two years ago, so this makes the third one I'm filling. We live in a tiny flat so crowded with family that a journal and the john are the only places a fella can find privacy.

Tomorrow it's back to school. If you ask me, school is jail for children, but it lets its prisoners out at three. As soon as we're free, nearly every fella I know heads for Newspaper Row. It's easy to find: Look for the tall gray buildings that house the newspaper offices on Park Row near City Hall. That's where all the important New York daily papers are published.

After school, Newspaper Row is crowded with fellas of all ages, waiting for the afternoon editions to come off the presses that rumble in the cellars of the newspaper office buildings. A fella can see *Evening Journal* newsies like myself, *World* newsies, *Times* newsies, *Sun* newsies, *Tribune* newsies, and more.

Some newsies I know cheat their customers by stretching the truth or making up headlines just to sell newspapers. They make up headlines like "Extra! Extra! Read all about it! White House scandal!" or "Big Gun Battle in Mullen's Pub!" By the time the customer realizes he's been suckered, he's blocks away, sitting on a train or trolley, or he's home eating his dinner.

Not me. I'm not one of those newsies because I hate it when someone lies to me. And I don't pull dodges that cheat customers out of their change because I hate it when somebody cheats me. Customers like it when a newsie's reliable, so no matter the weather, they can count on me to be at my corner.

I'm a newsie you can trust. Someday I'll be a reporter you can trust. All a fella's got to do is watch and listen carefully. And write everything down. Just like a reporter, really.

Monday, January 2, 1899

School. Not much I want to say about that except that our jailer is Mr. Henry Drinker, a tall, slim, bony, fault-finding man who starts each day the same way. Miserably.

School rules are worse than prison rules. Mr. Drinker is more stern than a prison guard. There are rules against using the johnny closet. Rules against staring out the window. Rules against talking to one another.

On Newspaper Row, there are no adults to breathe down our necks. We drink coffee, bolt hot dogs, throw dice, pitch pennies, and pelt one another with snowballs in City Hall Park. When the circulation bell rings and the circulation manager yells, "Newsies, get your papers!" we get down to business.

Tonight I stood in line behind my best friend, Racetrack Higgins, who sells more *Evening Journals* than any newsie I know. Since all I've got are sisters, Racetrack is the closest thing I know to a brother.

It was cold and snow was starting to fall. Racetrack had lined his coat with newspapers to stay warm, and he crackled each time he stamped his feet and blew into his hands. Older fellas like Kid Blink and Dave Simons elbowed their way to the front of the line and bought their papers first. It makes me mad the way they push their way around just because they're older.

When it was Racetrack's turn, he plunked sixty cents down and bought his usual number, one hundred papers. He grumbled to Mr. Needle, the circulation manager, about the cost. "For the life of me," said Racetrack, "I can't figure out why ten cents means that much to millionaires like Hearst and Pulitzer."

Racetrack can complain all he wants. It won't do any good. Last year, William Randolph Hearst, publisher of the *Evening Journal*, and Joseph Pulitzer, publisher of the *World*, raised the wholesale price of their newspapers ten cents. The customer still pays a penny a paper, but it costs us newsies sixty cents instead of fifty cents for one hundred papers. Mr. Hearst and Mr. Pulitzer are bitter rivals, always trying to outscoop each other. But the one thing they agree upon is how much they charge the newsies. It wasn't so bad last year during the Spanish-American War. Some nights *Journal* and *World* newsies sold seven or eight editions. But now the war is over and the news is tame. In a good week, I'm lucky to sell about three hundred papers.

"It's not personal, kid. It's business," said Mr. Needle.

"It feels personal," said Racetrack.

Then Mr. Needle shouted, "Next!"

It was my turn. I bought my usual fifty papers, nodded good-bye to Racetrack, and then started for my corner on New Chambers Street. It's a good corner, not far from

City Hall, where important-looking gents in derby hats and shined shoes pass as they head for the ferryboats and the trolley and train stations. Some gents hand me a nickel and don't even bother to wait for their four cents' change.

Some people might wonder why we don't sell one of the other newspapers, one that doesn't charge so much. The reason is simple: The *Journal* and the *World* outsell the other New York dailies. At quitting time, it's rush, rush, rush when thousands of factory and shop workers buy their papers as they head for home in the Lower East Side tenements.

I tucked the *Journals* under my arm. Two tired-looking men with dinner pails approached, and I shouted, "Read all about it! Man Arrested on Way to Murder Landlord!" They each dug into their pockets for a penny and bought a paper.

It sure isn't easy to shout a headline about your own grandfather, but it's not personal, I told myself. It's business. Before long, I had sold all but one *Journal*. That one I took home for Grandpa Jiggsy so that he could read about himself.

Later

It's not Grandpa Jiggsy's fault that he got hauled off to the cooler. Anyone who knows my grandfather knows that he sings when he drinks. He starts with his favorite ballads, which make him sad. Then he sings mournful songs about Ireland that make him mad. And then he sings rebel songs that build up the fight in him.

Most nights, Grandpa Jiggsy and Pop can be found at Lafferty's Pub on the Bowery. They sit at opposite ends of the bar, like complete strangers. It's my job to get them for supper on my way home from selling papers.

Before I got there last night, Grandpa Jiggsy had downed several shots and started singing. The barkeep, new on the job, told Grandpa Jiggsy to pipe down. Not one to pipe down, Grandpa Jiggsy climbed onto his chair and belted out, "'I'll be the man to lead the van beneath the flag of green!'"

Then he launched into a tirade about the landlord who evicted him and his family when he was a young boy in Ireland and how he'd like to kill that landlord. The barkeep sent for the cops.

When the cops arrived, they didn't want to arrest a man for singing, so they told him to pipe down, too. But Grandpa Jiggsy sang even louder.

I arrived in time to see two cops drag Grandpa Jiggsy

from his stool. The tall one pinned him to the floor while the shorter one frisked him. They didn't find a weapon, and the trouble might have ended there, except that the pat down insulted my grandfather. He popped to his feet and started jabbing.

Grandpa Jiggsy is sixty-two years old, but he's strong and wiry and still has great footwork. It took both cops and a couple of nudges with their nightsticks to get him into the paddy wagon. They took him to the county jail on Ludlow Street.

Meanwhile, a *Journal* reporter was sitting at the bar, hard-pressed for a headline. The reporter scribbled down the facts and improved them.

Pop said it would do Grandpa Jiggsy good to cool off for a day or two and give us some peace and quiet at home, but Ma wouldn't hear of it. She took money from her savings jar and paid Grandpa Jiggsy's two-dollar fine. Tonight when I got home from selling newspapers, he was home from jail, meek as a kitten. He hasn't so much as swiped sugar from the sugar bowl.

Tuesday, January 3, 1899

It's snowing again. Hard. Tonight, Grandpa Jiggsy burst inside our flat and hollered to Ma that he needed all the long underwear he could get. It turns out that my grandfather has got himself a job.

Excited, Grandpa Jiggsy told Ma that a gent who works for the city offered him work as snow foreman. It pays $1.40 a day. All he's got to do is round up forty hands to shovel the streets and sidewalks. They will each earn twelve and a half cents an hour, not bad pay for day labor.

Grandpa Jiggsy said to Pop, "You know what that means."

Pop didn't answer.

"I'm a boss," said Grandpa Jiggsy proudly.

"You're only a boss until the snow is cleared," Ma reminded Grandpa Jiggsy.

"Doesn't matter," said Grandpa Jiggsy. "I'm a boss." Then he said to Pop, "Maybe when you're my age, you'll be a boss, too."

Pop's face got scorched. If there's one thing that Pop has always wanted, it's to be a boss and make his own fortune. Pop says in America that anybody can be a boss. The only problem is that Pop has been in America nearly twenty years and he's still just a factory worker. Pop works at the cigarette factory on Cherry Street, where he rolls cigarettes six days a week, from six in the morning till six at night.

Before Pop said anything, Ma stepped in. "Hush your mouth," she told Grandpa Jiggsy, and her eyes meant it.

Pop grabbed his coat and stomped out, probably to find a beer hall. I waited till things quieted down, and then I whispered to Grandpa Jiggsy, "Give me a job. I want to shovel snow."

Some days Ma doesn't hear a word I say. Other days she has dog ears. "You are going to school," she said.

School, my arse, I wanted to say. But I can't say that. Not to Ma. So I said, "I'm thirteen. I'm old enough to do more than hawk newspapers. Even the law says so."

"Old enough, your arse," said Ma. "I did not bring you into this world to shovel snow. You're going to school, and that's that."

Sometimes Ma's mouth shocks us all.

Later

It's nearly nine o'clock. It's dark and still snowing hard. As far as I can see, squares of yellow light glow in tenement windows up and down the street. Broken talk filters through the thin walls of our flat. Somewhere supper dishes are rattling and two men are arguing.

On the parlor sofa, my sister Maggie has drawn the blanket over her head. She keeps whining that she can't sleep until I turn out the kerosene light and stop all my loud scratching in this journal. Maggie hates sharing the parlor with Grandpa Jiggsy and me, even though we sleep on the floor and she gets the sofa.

Ma sided with Maggie and told me to hurry up because Maggie has work tomorrow and needs her sleep. It's no use arguing with Ma because the only last words a person gets with her are "I'm sorry." So I'll just get the last word here: New York law says that twelve is old enough for a fella to work, as long as he attends school eighty days each year. At fourteen, a fella can quit school for good, as long as he has a job.

And that's what I intend to do, the day I turn fourteen, next August. I just haven't told Ma.

Wednesday, January 4, 1899

Grandpa Jiggsy was the first one up this morning. I listened to him dress in the dark: the thump of his feet as he pulled on his pants, the click of his belt buckle, the snap of his suspenders. In the kitchen, he kindled the stove fire, made his tea, and cut bread for his toast. Humming, he scraped his butter knife across the toast.

Ma heard the sugar bowl lid clink and she called out sleepily, "Easy on the sugar, Da. We ain't millionaires, you know." Ma always says that about sugar.

Grandpa Jiggsy called back, "Don't you worry, Clare.

When I get paid, we'll have plenty of sugar." The chair creaked as he bent over to lace his boots. Then the flat door opened and closed, and his deep voice boomed in the hallway.

Grandpa Jiggsy always talks in a shout. "Hallo there, Charlie. Look at all that snow outside. Need a job?"

That's when I remembered I was mad at Ma for making me go to school. I pulled the blanket over my head and wished for a stomachache or toothache or fever, anything at all to keep me home from school. But Ma wants proof. Even if I could make myself throw up, that wouldn't be proof enough. For Ma, you've got to throw up twice and have a fever to go with it. I ruled out a toothache because there was the danger Ma would pull it on me.

Around me, the tenement started to wake up. In the flat behind us, Mr. Sanko began to cough up his morning lumps. The fretful Sanko baby squalled. Overhead, feet thumped across the wooden floors. A sewing machine began to treadle. Across the hall, Mr. DePalma started to yell. Mrs. DePalma screamed back at him. They fight like cats, always sounding as though they're killing each other.

Ma soldiered Pop from the bedroom doorway. "Get up, Johnny," she said, "before you're late for work and find yourself fired."

My little sisters, Annie and Winnie, woke up fussy. Ma

shushed them as she changed their diapers. Pop staggered from the bedroom. He grabbed a handful of newspaper squares and headed downstairs to the johnny closet.

Then Maggie got up. She stepped over me and dashed herself with cold water in the kitchen. All without a word. Since she turned seventeen, she never has much to say unless she's pointing out a way a person can improve himself.

I waited till Pop and Maggie left, and then I got up. Ma had tea and buttered sugar toast waiting for me when I got back from the johnny closet. She was trying to make up for sending me to school, I could tell. "Sit," she said. "It ain't good to eat standing up. Drink your tea. When it's this cold outside, you need something warm inside." She pinched extra sugar onto my toast.

Ma mashed bread and banana with milk for Winnie and Annie. I gulped my tea and gobbled my toast. Then I grabbed my coat from the hook and shoved my arms through the sleeves. Ma handed me a scarf and hat. "Wear these," she said, pulling up my coat collar.

I hate it when Ma hovers over me like I'm six. She held out her cheek for me to kiss her. It shouldn't make a fella mad to kiss his mother good-bye, but some days it does. I ignored her and pretended I didn't see her hurt look. I grabbed my books and ran down the stairs.

Outside, the streets were covered with several inches of snow, and it was still falling. At the corner, a group of boys my age carried shovels and yelled to one another in Italian. Lucky dogs! Why couldn't Ma let me play hooky for just one day? One lousy day.

Some days I'm so sick to death of Ma, it makes me want to gnaw on my own leg.

Later

As always, school began with a roar. "Good morning!" Mr. Drinker bellowed from the doorway.

We leaped to our feet and snapped to attention, our backs straight as ramrods, eyes front, hands straight at our sides. "Good morning, Mr. Drinker," we chorused, all fifty-two of us.

Mr. Drinker nodded and we sank into our seats.

His eyes roved over us all. Lingering at Racetrack's empty seat, he lectured us on the importance of attendance. For the millionth time, he reminded us that the city superintendent will examine us in June to make sure we know our lessons. Once again, we heard how our promotion to seventh grade depends upon our performance. What he didn't say is this: *His* promotion depends upon our performance, too. We all know that Mr. Drinker longs to teach a higher grade.

Mr. Drinker crashed his pointer against a map of the United States and said we'd better know all forty-five states and their capitals, and by God, we'd better spell them right.

He crossed over to the blackboard, where our twenty spelling words were written. He struck the words with his pointer and told us to copy them in our best penmanship and, by God, we'd better know them. Copy them ten, no, Crash! make that twenty times each for tomorrow.

My second-best friend, Jimmy Vaskey, sits in the second row. A husky fella with brown hair, Jimmy doesn't have much going for him in the way of talent except for a friendly face. I feel sorry for him because he takes longer to catch on. He gets his times tables mixed up, he can't read without stumbling over the words, and his handwriting is a mess, his letters squashed together in his copybook. Still, nobody tries harder than Jimmy.

Jimmy reached for his copybook. Mr. Drinker sprang upon him. Crash! He slammed his pointer down onto Jimmy's desk. "Did I say now?" Mr. Drinker hollered.

Jimmy tried to stammer an answer, but Mr. Drinker's pointer crashed again. "Make that thirty times each for you, Mr. Vaskey."

"N-n-now?" asked Jimmy.

"No, not now!" said Mr. Drinker.

Mr. Drinker worked himself into a frenzy. He called us a bunch of good-for-nothings who couldn't follow simple directions. Then he popped two peppermints into his mouth and chewed them to settle his stomach.

Thursday, January 5, 1899

Another miserable day in school. Still no sign of Racetrack. Mr. Drinker lectured us again on the importance of attendance.

Racetrack is what teachers call a bad influence, because he doesn't follow rules made by other people. He follows his own rules. For instance, he says you should live each day as though it's your last and someday you'll be right. He says never dare someone to do something that you would not dare to do yourself. But his most important rule is this: He says never feel sorry for any grown-up who gets duped by a kid because grown-ups are older and should know better.

Racetrack's brain drives Mr. Drinker crazy because he can't understand how a fella who misses so much school can be so smart. Racetrack can add columns of numbers and multiply by two digits in his head. He can hear something once and remember it. If Racetrack has a downfall, it's tests because he mixes up letters and numbers and words on paper. He does things his own way, not Mr. Drinker's.

I don't like taking tests because it feels as though I'm showing someone the inside of my brain. But, like tests or not, I'm good at them and I make good grades, some of the highest in the class. I guess I'm smart, but I don't always use my head for common sense.

Later

No sign of Racetrack on Newspaper Row either.

When I got home from selling papers, Ma was singing songs about dear little shamrocks and the last rose of summer as she diced the potatoes and sliced the carrots into circles. Cooking always makes Ma sing.

Ma buys groceries for pennies at a time — three cents' worth of sugar, five cents' worth of butter, five cents' worth of tea, ten cents' worth of chicken, everything in pennies. Any way she can, Ma scrounges. She walks blocks to buy soup bones a penny cheaper and bread a half cent less. Ma says a penny saved is a penny earned.

But Grandpa Jiggsy has a job and he's earned boss's wages. The streets are cleared, and it's payday. To celebrate, Ma splurged on potatoes, turnips, carrots, and cabbage from the Italian grocer, and beef from the German butcher. Ma won't buy on credit because she says there's nothing worse than owing money and being beholden to someone.

Just as I hung up my coat, the door flew open and Grandpa Jiggsy stomped inside. Snow flew off his hat and coat. He tossed a round brass tag onto the kitchen table. "That no-good cuss promised to pay us, but this voucher is all we got," he said disgustedly.

"When will you get paid?" Ma asked.

"Don't know," said Grandpa Jiggsy. And he told us how some fathead who works for the city came around and offered to buy the workers' vouchers for half their value if men needed money in a hurry.

Grandpa Jiggsy smacked his fist against his hand and said, "I wanted to punch him in the nose. I wised up my fellas, but some sold their vouchers anyway. The poor fellas were desperate to put food on their tables."

Ma took a deep breath. I knew she was thinking about the savings money she had spent on our supper.

Friday, January 6, 1899

Grandpa Jiggsy has made the headlines! And this time it had nothing to do with cops or the cooler!

I rushed home to show Ma, but Grandpa Jiggsy had already spread out a *Journal* on the kitchen table.

Right there in bold letters the headline read, "Snow Shovelers Want Their Pay." Beneath that, a photograph showed a group of men. Grandpa Jiggsy jabbed his index finger at his face in the photograph. "I'm famous."

Grandpa Jiggsy told us how the snow shovelers had gathered outside the city paymaster's office at 35 New Chambers Street, where they'd complained loudly about not receiving their promised wages. When they hadn't gotten any satisfaction from the paymaster, Grandpa Jiggsy had marched the shovelers to the *Journal* offices on Park Row and explained the men's plight to a reporter. In the article, the reporter called the situation a "grave injustice."

"A boss has to look out for his workers," said Grandpa Jiggsy. He jabbed at the top of another head in the photograph. "Know this young fella?"

I couldn't tell.

"It's your pal, Racetrack. He found a dead man over on Seventh Street," said Grandpa Jiggsy. "Poor stiff was frozen solid beneath a wagon."

Racetrack, the lucky dog! No wonder he hasn't been in school. My liver burned with envy.

Saturday, January 7, 1899

I made twenty cents plus a nickel in tips last night. I kept the tips for myself but gave the earnings to Ma.

Ma reached for the jam jar that she keeps hidden in the kitchen cupboard. She twisted off the lid and dropped in the change. It's our savings jar.

We're luckier than most Bowery families because we have savings. We don't have to share our three-room flat with anyone except Grandpa Jiggsy. Other families we know take in boarders and rent out their tiny rooms with two or three families. Most boarders are new immigrants who don't speak English. I see them in the morning, looking pale and bewildered as they stand around in their baggy foreign underwear, scratching and waiting their turn for the john.

We all do what we can to help pay the rent, put food on the table, and add money to our savings jar. In a good week, I make about a dollar twenty selling papers.

Maggie works at the pants factory on Ludlow Street and makes about six dollars a week. Each night she brings home pants for Ma to finish by hand. During the day, Ma sews canvas around the bottom of each pant leg, inserts linings into the waistband, tacks pockets, fastens stays and buttons, makes buttonholes, attaches buckles to a back strap, and sews on merchandise tickets. Ma earns seven cents for each pair of pants. If Ma has a good week, she makes about two dollars.

Pop has been working regular at the cigarette factory for nearly a year now. When he comes home, his fingers are stained brown and he smells sweet like tobacco. He makes about eight dollars a week.

Grandpa Jiggsy finds odd jobs and scavenges coal from the rail yard and scrap lumber that we burn in our kitchen stove. Pop won't scavenge, not even when he's between jobs. He says it's not respectable for a man who intends to be a boss. He says a man who scrounges is not a man. He's a beggar.

Each time the savings jar becomes filled, Ma carries it to the Bowery Savings Bank, where it's growing into the house Pop says we'll buy someday.

Sunday, January 8, 1899

It's been a long time since I've thought about our some-day house. One Sunday, when I was seven, Pop rented an open four-wheel carriage and two horses. Ma packed a picnic lunch — bread, cheese, pickles, hard-boiled eggs, and bananas — and we all piled into the carriage.

Pop snapped the reins and we rattled down the Bowery

streets, all the way to the Brooklyn Bridge. As we crossed the bridge, the wide East River flowed beneath us, dotted with boats of all sizes. On the other side, tall buildings jutted up like jagged teeth against the sky. Smoke rose from the factory smokestacks along the waterfront.

We rode until the Brooklyn buildings gave way to small houses, grass, dirt, and trees. Soon we came to a white clapboard house with an elm tree in the front yard and blue flowers creeping up a white picket fence. "Morning glories," said Ma with a longing in her voice. I had never seen flowers the color of Ma's eyes before.

Pop pulled back the reins, and the horses stopped. He squeezed Ma's hand and we looked at those flowers and that house for the longest time. I knew Pop and I were thinking the same thing: how much we'd like to give Ma a pretty little white house and morning glories someday.

That Christmas, Pop gave Ma a china plate. On the plate he had painted morning glories. The flowers looked so real that Ma said they smelled beautiful. We all took turns sniffing the plate.

Now the blue-flowered plate sits in our parlor on a wooden mantel that Grandpa Jiggsy made from scrap lumber. If there was a fire in the middle of the night, the one thing Ma would save, after we were all safe, is that plate.

Monday, January 9, 1899

Another miserable school day. At least Racetrack was there, sitting in the back row. He had washed his face and brushed his dark hair so that it was slicked in place, which gave him a tough look. I wish I looked tough like Racetrack.

As Mr. Drinker took roll, he noted Racetrack's attendance and said, "How nice of you to grace us with your presence, Mr. Higgins."

Racetrack seemed to enjoy the sarcasm. His dark eyes danced as he said, "Thank you, sir. It's good to be in school." That's another tough thing about Racetrack: his smile. It's part friendly, part I-dare-you.

Mr. Drinker fired question after question at Racetrack — history, math, and spelling. I felt pumped up with excitement as Racetrack returned fire, answer for answer. He didn't miss one.

By the afternoon, Mr. Drinker was popping peppermints like nobody's business. He chomped them, one after the other. He began our math lesson with a review of the times tables, which I knew by heart but fellas like Jimmy did not.

Mr. Drinker told us that we had better know our times tables, by God, frontwards, backwards, and sideways. And if he catches us using our fingers for the ninees, he'll cut them off. He tells us he has a finger-chopping machine in his closet, and by God! he'll use it. We'll go the rest of our lives with nine fingers, and by God! we believe him.

Jimmy Vaskey raised his hand. "What?" barked Mr. Drinker.

"Sir, how do you use your fingers for the nineses?" Jimmy asked simply. We all looked at one another and wondered if Jimmy was trying to commit suicide.

Mr. Drinker's eyes bulged, but Jimmy kept on. "I'd like to know, sir, because I want to be sure not to do it."

Mr. Drinker pounced on Jimmy and dragged him by the collar to the front of the room. He yanked open his closet door. We sat wide-eyed, certain that Mr. Drinker would pull out the finger-chopping machine. We leaned forward for a closer look.

Instead, Mr. Drinker grabbed his long wooden paddle from its hook on the closet door. Whack! Whack! he walloped Jimmy's backside. "Now, stop your foolish questions and sit down," said Mr. Drinker.

Head down, Jimmy returned to his seat. Mr. Drinker popped another peppermint and said to us, "Who else wants to know how to do the nineses on his fingers?"

Tuesday, January 10, 1899

We stood outside the school today, trying to persuade Jimmy to go in. He did not want to see Mr. Drinker.

To make Jimmy feel better, I told him that a paddling is no big deal. "With Mr. Drinker, it's always two whacks, never more, never less," I said.

Jimmy said, "That's easy for you to say. You never catch it."

"It's just a matter of time before we all catch it," said Grin Boyle.

Racetrack agreed and added, "When I catch it, I bet I can get more than two whacks out of Mr. Drinker."

That cracked us up, the way Racetrack will bet on anything, even his own paddling. We took him up on the bet, and I have two bits riding on it, in Racetrack's favor. Mr. Drinker and Racetrack have been circling each other like tomcats since the beginning of the year.

We pushed open the heavy doors and went inside.

Later

I guess you could call the five of us — Racetrack, Jimmy, Grin Boyle, Mush Myers, and me — a gang because we hang out together.

Everything is a joke to Grin Boyle. That fella's always in trouble for foolishness, mostly because he can't stop himself from grinning. It makes Mr. Drinker think he's up to something even when he's not.

Mush is the kind of fella that girls watch go by. We're nearly the same height, but he's got a better build, more shoulders, and muscles all the way up to his neck. He's always got a girl, which is why the fellas call him Mush.

Every fella I know belongs to a gang, mostly for protection. Ask anybody and they'll tell you that the Bowery district is a tough place to live. It can be suicide to leave your block because each block is its own country, ruled by a different gang. A fella learns fast who lives where and what answers to give when toughs pop up out of nowhere and ask what street you're from. Say the wrong street, and Bang! you're jumped and beat up with sticks, stones, fists, and feet. Your lip is split. Your eye black. And your money, if you had any, stolen.

A fella also learns to carry some sort of boodle when he's out by himself — a penny, an empty spool, a dead ball, anything at all to buy his freedom if he gets jumped. It doesn't cost much. It's mostly a matter of paying a gang the proper respect.

If I had to say who our leader was, I'd say Racetrack. He's not the biggest fella, but size doesn't matter in a fight. He has a toughness that makes fellas follow him.

When he speaks, he can sway fellas to see his side in any argument. Racetrack is my age, thirteen, but he seems older, probably because he has it rough at home. His father is dead, and his stepmother is a hard woman who throws him out when he wears down her nerves. When she does, he usually stays at the Newsboys' Lodging House on Duane Street until he can't take their rules anymore.

As far as fighting goes, I'm lucky to have Grandpa Jiggsy. He taught me everything I need to know. He says a good fight is all in the feet, because the punch follows the feet. By the time I was six, I knew how to jab, feint, bob and weave, cross with my right, then cut with a left hook.

- Make a good tight knuckle fist. Wrap your thumb around your fingers.
- Throw from the shoulder.
- Drive each punch by turning the wrist like a corkscrew.
- Go for the face, because most fellas protect their faces, especially if they're pretty.
- Stay on your feet. Don't be the first to fall.
- If you do fall, pop back up. Don't roll into a ball, thinking you're going to protect yourself. You won't.

- Once you decide to fight, don't quit. A fight isn't over till it's over. There is no enough. Say you hit a guy and he goes down. You go down on top of him. Don't let him get back up.

Thursday, January 12, 1899

It is so cold that the three lakes at Central Park have frozen over. The Park Department engineers tested the ice and raised a red ball over the lake this morning to let people know it is safe for skating.

That makes Grandpa Jiggsy laugh. He says leave it to the city to think they need to pay engineers to tell when the ice is safe. He says you can tell the ice is packing when it makes sharp pistol-like snaps during the night.

It costs twenty-five cents to rent skates at Central Park, so the fellas and I stick to the frozen ponds in the Lower East Side, where a fella can skate in his shoes.

Saturday, January 14, 1899

Saturdays are the best days, the days the gang goes junking. This morning, the fellas and I combed the alleys and streets and junk heaps for rags, paper, bottles, cans, and other luck to sell to the junkman. He paid a penny for ten pounds of paper, two cents for one pound of rags, and four cents for one pound of iron. We pooled the pennies and spent them at Haber's candy store.

Wednesday, January 18, 1899

I had sold the last of my newspapers tonight and was headed home when somebody shouted, "Fire at Cammeyer's!" Cammeyer's is a six-story uptown department store on the corner of Sixth Avenue and Twentieth Street.

An uptown fire is always big news. I ran back to Newspaper Row to watch the story break. All along Newspaper Row, *Journal* reporters rushed out, pulling on their coats as they ran. They tripped over one another to be the first to reach the disaster scene.

No newspaper scoops the *Journal*. Mr. Hearst spares no expense if it means he'll beat out the *World* and other papers. If Mr. Pulitzer sends ten men, Mr. Hearst will send twenty. Sometimes Mr. Hearst sends so many reporters, he has no one left if another story breaks. But it doesn't matter to Mr. Hearst: He can hire freelance reporters who sit on benches in City Hall Park or in the nearby bars.

When the story's big enough, rich Mr. Hearst himself leads the charge. Tonight he stood outside the *Journal* office, shouting orders, barking commands, and gesturing signals.

His reporters hailed hansom cabs and captured bicycles from messenger and delivery boys. Outriders jumped onto bicycles and sped ahead on the slippery snow-covered streets, shouting to make way for the *Journal* carriages. The cavalcade careened up Park Row, leaving the other newspaper reporters to follow. Then Mr. Hearst himself leaped long-legged into his private carriage and was whisked away like a field marshal to the scene of battle.

I can't stop thinking about those reporters. It must feel glorious to be the gent who writes the news instead of the poor sucker who stands on street corners shouting the headlines. Some day that gent will be me.

Thursday, January 19, 1899

Sold seventy-five papers tonight, thanks to last night's fire. People love to read about disaster. Racetrack sold one hundred and fifty and said he could have doubled his sales if someone had died in the fire. It shocked me, hearing him say that. He told me I have to toughen up. I suppose he's right, especially if I want to be a reporter.

Monday, January 23, 1899

Tonight Racetrack coached a small boy in the art of newspaper selling. The boy, still in knee pants, didn't look much more than nine, the same age I started as a newsie.

Racetrack put his arm around the boy's shoulders and pointed to the huge signboard high up on the *Journal* building, where two men standing on a balcony chalked the day's headlines.

Racetrack scanned the signboard. "First, you find a headline worth shouting," he told the boy. "Too bad there wasn't another fire like the other night. Or an earthquake or murder." He thought a moment and then said, "Try this one: 'Man Bites Dog!' That headline's guaranteed to sell papers, or my name ain't Racetrack Higgins."

That cracked me up. Sometimes I think Racetrack forgets that his real name is Thomas.

The boy squinted at the signboard. "It doesn't say anything about a man biting a dog there."

Racetrack grew impatient. "Listen, kid, do you want to sell papers or not?"

The boy nodded. "Then remember this," said Racetrack.

"A dog that bites a man is not news. But a man who bites a dog, now that's a story that will sell newspapers."

The boy drew in a deep breath and hollered, "Man bites dog!"

"Good," said Racetrack to the boy. "Now, remember these things: Always call a gent 'sir,' especially those gents who look like they've been bossed around all day. Always tip your hat to a lady and say, 'Thank you, ma'am.'"

Taking a step back, he sized up the boy from head to toe. "I'd say you're good for twenty-five papers." He handed the boy fifteen cents. "Tomorrow you pay me back, plus a nickel."

The boy thanked Racetrack and hurried back to his friends. Racetrack caught me looking at him. "Don't look at me like that," he said. "I ain't doing nothing those yellow reporters don't do. And besides, I did the kid a favor. A nickel ain't much to pay for front money and an education. Besides, I threw in the headline for free."

Racetrack is right. The *Journal* and the *World* are called "yellow" newspapers because their reporters sensationalize the facts. The more exclamation points a headline has, the better. For fire, the headline screams, "Flames!" For a collision, "Crash!!" For murder, "Blood!!!"

Mr. Drinker criticizes the yellow newspapers. He says that a newspaper is a public servant and that it should never pander or compromise. He says that reading yellow newspapers like the *Journal* and the *World* is like watching a train wreck and hoping you'll see a body. He prefers the more flavorsome writing of the New York *Sun*.

When I'm a reporter, I'll be one you can trust. I'll write for the New York *Sun* or the *New York Times*. For now I sell the *Journal* because I want to help Ma get her someday house. That's not business. That's personal.

Wednesday, February 1, 1899

Our landlord, Mr. Underman, came by to collect our rent tonight, and Ma complained again about the water pump in the backyard. It's been blocked for two months now. She told him that it's not right that the tenants have to carry buckets to the street and search for a pump where they can get water.

Mr. Underman jotted himself a note and promised to send his man around to fix the plumbing. Then he took our rent money, checked off our names in his book, and left.

Here at Mott Street, we pay twelve dollars a month and for what? Five stories of crumbling red and black bricks. Dirty broken stairs. Dark hallways that smell like somebody uses them for a toilet. A three-room flat so choked with people that you feel as though you're holding your breath.

Next to Mr. Underman, our main enemy is the dirt. Ma leads charges against enemy fleas, cockroaches, and bedbugs. With her broom, she attacks the dirt and falling-down ceiling plaster. On her hands and knees, she scours our floors. She boils water and launders shirts, pants, underwear, socks, skirts, blouses, and diapers. She scrubs and rinses and wrings out our three sheets, three towels, and four washrags. Our flat always smells sour like under the arms, no matter how much Ma cleans. It's a losing battle, but Ma won't surrender.

On other streets, newer tenements have pipes that bring water right to the kitchen sink and two flush toilets on each floor. But not us. Our water pump is broken. Our johnny closet is an old privy that sits in the backyard, three flights down. It seats five, but it's shared by every family in the building. Some mornings a fella can't wait his turn. That's why grass never grows around the john.

Thursday, February 2, 1899

Even in winter, there's an eviction on every street. This morning, when cries and shouts rose up from the street below, Ma crossed herself and whispered a prayer for the evicted family. The city marshal and policemen carried out their household goods and set them on the sidewalk.

A young woman, hardly older than Maggie, sat huddled by her belongings. She cradled her baby and shivered in the cold. Her husband stood by helplessly, his hands in his pockets.

When I came home from school, I was not surprised to find the evicted family in our kitchen, sipping tea and slurping soup. Our parlor is filled with their belongings: trunks, boxes, a feather mattress, pottery, pots, pans, and strange-looking clothing. Ma said they will stay with us tonight and find a new flat tomorrow.

Pop says Ma has a knack for finding people in trouble, and he's right. It's never a surprise to come home and find some woman spilling out her troubles. Ma pours tea and listens, never telling them what to do unless they ask.

Friday, February 3, 1899

No good headlines to shout. I bought fifty papers but sold only forty-six. The four unsold papers aren't refundable, but they don't go to waste. After Pop is done reading and Maggie is done studying the latest fashions, Ma cuts them into square wipes for us to use in the johnny closet.

Saturday, February 4, 1899

Bath night. Maggie refused to help carry water because she said the heavy buckets hurt her hands and bump against her shins, leaving blue bruises.

Ma said Maggie does her share because she works at the pants factory, twelve hours a day, six days a week, and so my sister thinks she's won. Ma said carrying buckets will build my muscles and put shoulders on me.

After I made five trips up and down the stairs, I groaned and collapsed into a chair. Maggie rolled her eyes and said, "You're such a baby."

Ma heated the water on the stove. I dragged the icy tin tub from the fire escape and into the kitchen. Then I waited in the hall while Maggie bathed.

By the time it was my turn, the water was cold enough to freeze off my hind parts. My front parts, too. I gritted my teeth and squeezed myself into the tub. I felt like a cricket with my knees bent up around my ears.

Grandpa Jiggsy says he expects to get only two good baths in his lifetime. He got the first from the midwife the day he was born, and he'll get the second from the undertaker the day he dies.

Sunday, February 5, 1899

Grandpa Jiggsy didn't come home last night, so I had the parlor floor to myself.

This morning I was digging for my other sock behind the boxes stacked in the corner when I found a balled-up pair of brand-new silk hose.

I dangled the stockings in front of Maggie, still asleep, so that they touched her nose. Her eyes popped open. She snatched at the stockings, but I whipped them out of reach. She threatened to knock me out cold.

I told her she had to catch me first. I trailed the stockings around my neck and arms and did a dance, one that Racetrack and I'd seen a Bowery dance-hall woman do.

Maggie sprang at me again. She's quick. I'm quicker. I stuffed the stockings down my pants. "You're disgusting," said Maggie. "Why don't you grow up?"

"I'll give your stockings back," I said. "Right after I show them to Ma." I had Maggie and she knew it. Ma would pitch a fit if she knew Maggie had wasted good money on silk hose.

Maggie glowered. "You wouldn't."

"Care to negotiate?" I taunted.

Maggie hissed, "Yes."

I won. I won. I won. For my silence and her stockings,

Maggie has promised to help fetch bathwater for the rest of February.

Monday, February 6, 1899

This morning when Ma woke Pop for work, he rolled over and said, "Getting up this early makes me sick."

Ma told him getting up early wouldn't make him sick if he didn't stay out so late at *those* places.

I know the places Pop visits. They're places where pianos tinkle and hurdy-gurdies wheeze and men smoke fat cigars and play cards. In the morning, Pop's breath smells sour from whiskey.

Ma lowered her voice, but her whisper mingled sharply with Pop's softer tones. I don't know what Pop said, but he made Ma laugh, and all the sharp edges left her voice. She can never stay mad at Pop for long.

Then Winnie said, "Dadadadada." It always wins Pa over the way Winnie calls him and waves her arms to be picked up.

"That's my girl," said Pop.

Ma said, "Since she's your girl, you can change her diaper."

Pop won't scrounge coal or firewood, but he never

minds helping with the babies. As he changed Winnie, he sang to her about eyes that shine like diamonds. Then he danced Winnie around the kitchen and told her how lovely she and Annie and Maggie are and how lucky they are to look like Ma with their dark curly hair and blue eyes. I look like Pop.

He put on his white shirt and coat and hat. He kissed Ma and the girls good-bye and me, too. Pop says a son is never too old for a father to kiss. Ma watched him with shining eyes as he left for work, still singing.

That's the thing about Ma. She's crazy about Pop, no matter how he vexes her.

Later

The truth is that we're never going to buy a someday house because Pop doesn't hold on to a job long enough. No job suits Pop for long.

Before the tobacco factory, Pop worked at the chair factory on Cherry Street. Before that, the soap factory on Elizabeth Street. Before that, the hairbrush factory on Grand Street.

Pop won't dress like a common factory worker. No matter the job, he wears a white-collared shirt each day, the same white shirt that Ma rinses out each night. He says you never know when the boss will notice someone who has enough respect for himself to wear a collared shirt.

Pop is not long for the cigarette factory. I can see the signs already. Each morning, it gets harder for him to get out of bed. He complains that the bosses expect him to sweep up the floors and stack boxes. He says a man who wears a collared shirt should not have to do these things.

Wednesday, February 8, 1899

The Sanko baby died last night. Ma stayed up at their flat all day yesterday, cooking and cleaning and helping with the three other children. Ma came home tired and with red eyes. She said the two-year-old is doing poorly and no doubt will join her baby sister in Heaven soon.

It gives me a hollow feeling inside, hearing about sick and dying babies. It makes me think about my own two little brothers who died before they were big enough to play with.

Friday, February 10, 1899

More snow. More zero temperatures. It's so cold that ice floes float like small islands in the East River.

Grandpa Jiggsy said that he hasn't seen such a sight since the blizzard of 1888, when boats crashed into the ice floes and a temporary ice bridge formed across the East River, joining Brooklyn and Manhattan.

Saturday, February 11, 1899

This morning was zero cold out, and Racetrack wore so many rags to keep warm that he looked like a walking rag pile.

Racetrack leaned into us as we walked, changing our course past our usual junking haunts. We followed Broome Street out to the East River, and then turned south. We passed the lumberyards, the cigarette factory where Pop works, and the iron foundry along the waterfront. There's nothing colder than the wind coming off the East River. It stung my face and froze my eyelashes.

We walked past Corlear's Hook Park, where we built our fort last summer, and where Mush likes to brag that he kisses his girlfriends. Sometimes it makes me wonder what it would be like to kiss a girl. Other times it makes me want to smash him in the mouth.

Soon we were standing at the edge of Pier 54, watching the boats dodge the ice floes.

Racetrack said that, according to salvage laws, if a boat crashes into an ice floe and becomes abandoned by its captain and crew, it's first come, first served. It amazes me how Racetrack always knows things like that.

Jimmy said that we'd be pirates. We decided that pirates need a flag, so we scouted around until we found a black rag and tied it to a stick. From the pier, we cheered the ice floes as boats charged them at full speed. Each time, we hoped for a boat to crash.

But by noon, most boats were safe at their slips. Not one had crashed, and we felt numb with cold. We gave up and headed toward Newspaper Row, where we each drank a bowl of coffee to warm up.

Tuesday, February 14, 1899

Today was Valentine's Day and it made me wish I had a girlfriend. I haven't had a girlfriend since third grade, when I ate a worm to prove my love to Rebecca Caughey. She called me a disgusting creature and dropped me.

Ma reminded us that tomorrow is Ash Wednesday, a day of fasting and the beginning of Lent. Ma has decided that we will give up sugar for Lent. She said we will put the pennies we save in the poor box at church. Pop suggested that we could add the pennies to our savings jar, but Ma said no, that would be selfish and nothing good comes out of selfishness.

"Speaking of selfishness," I said, looking at Maggie. I held up my leg and trailed my fingers, as if I were pulling on stockings.

Maggie tightened her face and sent me a death stare. If her eyes were knives, I'd have been stabbed. I clutched my hand over my heart. "Acckk," I said. "You're killing me." I toppled off my chair and fell onto the floor.

"What in the world has gotten into him?" said Ma.

Saturday, February 18, 1899

I no sooner got home from selling newspapers last night than Ma handed me her black frypan and told me to hurry to the fishmonger on Elizabeth Street to buy a panful of herring for supper.

I told Ma that it's not right for a fella to run through the streets carrying a frypan like a girl. Ma thought that over and then handed me an extra penny to use as boodle in case a gang jumped me.

I told Ma it's not right for a mother to give her son boodle, as though she thinks he can't take care of himself. But Ma gave me one of her looks and there's no arguing with her eyes, so I took the penny and said, "How much fish?"

I bought the fish and headed home. It was dark. The wind stung my face, and I wished I'd worn a hat and gloves. Suddenly, I heard feet behind me, and I got a feeling I didn't like. The feet sounded too steady to belong to drunks, so they could only mean one thing: a couple of toughs looking for a fight.

I picked up my pace, wondering if I should cheese it and run or turn and fight. I've been in plenty of fights, but I'd never been jumped alone. I remembered how Jimmy got jumped last summer. He got beat up pretty badly.

The feet quickened behind me. I gripped the frypan handle tighter and felt my heart beating in my ears. Not wanting to get jumped from behind, I spun around to face my attackers.

It was Racetrack and Mush! "You're running like you stole something," said Mush. Racetrack laughed because he knows I don't steal.

Racetrack and Mush live in the same tenement, two blocks over on Mulberry, so they walked me home. We passed a construction site where a new tenement is going up. Inside a small shanty, the watchman sat close to his woodstove, fast asleep, his fingers laced across his broad stomach.

It doesn't take much to give Mush ideas. "Watch this," he said. He sneaked over to the shack and scaled its side, quick and strong, like a cat. The watchman never stirred.

I'm not going to write down what Mush did, but I will say this: No grass will grow on top of that shack. Poof! Gray and white steam shot up the stovepipe. Inside, the shack must have smelled something awful! The watchman snapped awake and charged outside, roaring like a bull.

Mush leaped from the roof. "Cheese it!" he yelled, and ran.

Racetrack sped off, but I stood there, holding the frypan and laughing. That's what I mean about not using my head for common sense. Because I wasn't guilty, I didn't run.

Seeing me, the watchman rushed over and grabbed me by the collar. He pulled me close to his face. His breath was practically inflammable. "I'll teach wise guys like you to respect the property of others!" he hollered. He swore at me and then boxed both sides of my head. His blows knocked me out cold for a full minute.

The next thing I knew, Racetrack was bending over me, worried. "You okay, pal?" he asked.

I felt pretty dazed, but I could see he felt terrible.

"I thought you were a goner," said Racetrack. "You scared me half to death." He helped me to my feet.

The scattered herring stared at me with dull, stupid eyes. Knowing Ma would be furious if I lost our supper, I reached to pick them up. The ground wavered.

Racetrack caught me before I toppled over. "Forget the fish," he said. "Let's get you home."

I leaned against Racetrack and we stumbled home. As soon as Ma saw my bruised face and her fingers touched the goose egg on my head, she demanded to know what happened. Racetrack can lie to anybody except Ma. He told her, Mush, stovepipe, and all.

Ma took a deep breath. I knew she wanted to lecture me about the company I keep. But she didn't. She knew I'd stick up for Mush no matter what, because that's the way a gang has to be. She wrapped herself in her black shawl and said, "I suppose if we want supper, I'll need my fish." She said the words matter-of-factly, as if she were going to the fishmonger's.

Ma's got little feet, but bam bam bam those feet stomped down all three flights of stairs. When Ma's mad, she walks like she's got a load on her back.

Racetrack leaped up and said he'd help her. When they came home, Ma had the black frypan and the fish, all neatly cleaned. Racetrack gazed hungrily at the fish. Ma never minds an extra mouth for dinner, and she told Racetrack to wash his hands and face if he intended to sit at our table. Without another word, she whisked around the kitchen, cooking dinner.

My head hurts. More later.

Later

At dinner, Racetrack told how Ma marched over to the watchman's shanty and yanked open the door. There stood the watchman, frying our fish!

Ma demanded the return of her frypan and our dinner.

"You're crazy," said the watchman.

"If you want to keep the nose on your face, you'd better mind how you talk to a lady," said Ma.

With a laugh, the watchman said, "What lady?"

At that, Ma tightened her fist and pow! She sent a blow to the watchman's kisser. He reeled backward. The whole shanty shook as he fell. "That's for my son," she said. "The next time you pick on someone, you'd better make sure he's guilty." Then she grabbed the frypan and our supper and left.

I whistled. It was Ma's best fight ever. But Maggie rolled her eyes and said, "Ma, if you want to be treated like a lady, you need to act like a lady."

Pop didn't laugh. He told Ma that she shouldn't take matters like these into her own hands, that she should have found a policeman and reported the watchman.

Grandpa Jiggsy kissed the top of Ma's head. "That's my girl," he said. "Did you remember to turn your fist like a corkscrew?"

Sunday, February 19, 1899

My best fight happened in fourth grade, the year I met Racetrack. His first day at school, he used a bad word. The teacher washed out his mouth with yellow soap and then stood him in the corner. I liked Racetrack immediately.

Then one day Racetrack and I were shooting marbles, and words led to insults and insults led to a push and a push led to fists. The other kids shouted, "Fight! Fight! Fight!" and ringed around us.

I put my head down and tore into Racetrack, fists flying. Blood spurted from his nose. He hooked his arm around my neck and drove a fist into my jaw. I fell but dragged him down with me. Over and over, we rolled on the ground, kicking and punching. Peddlers, deliverymen, and mothers came running. A woman shrieked, "These boys are killing each other! Where are their mothers!"

"I'm right here," said Ma. And she was, right in the front row, cheering me on, yelling things like, "Turn your fist!" Ma knew we had to finish that fight. She says running away never does anyone any good.

I didn't win that day, but I held my own. Racetrack gave me a black eye and I gave him a bloody nose. Ma took a nickel from the savings jar and made me and

Racetrack the best steak dinner we ever had. That day, Racetrack and I became best friends.

Thursday, February 23, 1899

The closer rent day comes, the louder the women complain about the broken pump. This afternoon they crowded into our flat, overflowing into the hall.

The women were talking wildly about Mr. Underman. When they were done with him, there would be nothing left but his shoes.

Mrs. Sanko said we should all move out and leave Mr. Underman with an empty building to fill.

Nobody liked that idea. "It's too much trouble to move," said Mrs. Brzowski. "Our husbands must be near their work. We cannot afford streetcar fare."

"Why should we move when it's our landlord who doesn't make repairs?" said Mrs. Leiberman, a tiny, fidgety woman, barely five feet tall.

"Let's give him something to repair," said Mrs. Peduto. "Let's smash out the windows! Let's hack out the walls!"

Mrs. DePalma looked at Ma. "What do you think, Clare?"

Ma said it's not right to destroy property that belongs to someone else, even a man like Mr. Underman. It only creates more trouble, and trouble has a way of following you.

"But what can we do?" asked another woman.

"We can stick together," said Ma. "Rent day is next week. We can refuse to pay until repairs are made."

"You mean a rent strike?" said Mrs. DePalma. Her eyes brightened. I could tell she liked the idea.

"A rent strike," Ma said, nodding her head.

Excited, the women all chattered at once. When Mr. Underman comes to collect the rent, they agreed they will refuse to pay until repairs are made.

Later

Pop doesn't like the idea of a rent strike. He told Ma that she should go to City Hall or to the Board of Health and complain.

Ma told him that City Hall officials don't listen to people who live in Bowery tenements.

"Then we'll move," Pop said.

But Ma doesn't want to move. It costs money to move. The cheap flats are filled, and the better flats cost too much money. She doesn't want to leave Mott Street, where all her friends live. The women here need her, she said. She doesn't want to abandon them.

Pop told her that it's a dog-eat-dog world out there, and that if you want to get ahead, you have to worry about yourself, not everyone else. "Nothing good can come out of a rent strike," he said.

Ma told Pop that we must stand up for our rights. She said that the tenants have right on their side.

Knowing Ma's mind was made up, Pop sighed and said, "Mark my words, Clare. Mr. Underman is too powerful. He has too much pull at City Hall."

Monday, February 27, 1899

This morning I nearly bowled over Mr. Underman, who was standing outside our door, his hand raised ready to knock. He came to collect the rent. Two days early.

"The cockroaches are getting more polite," said Grandpa Jiggsy. "This one knocks."

Ma looked Mr. Underman in the eye, saying, "It's been three months and our plumbing is still not fixed."

Annoyance flickered across Mr. Underman's face, but he forced a smile. He took out his little notebook and scribbled something down and said, "There, I have made myself a note. My man will be around next week."

Ma told him, "Three times you have said next week, and next week turns into next month."

Mr. Underman bristled with anger, but he composed

himself and said, "Sorry, lady, but I'm a busy man." He tapped his brown notebook with his pencil as he waited in our doorway.

Ma balled her hands into fists on her hips. "It's not right that we are paying rent," she said, "and you are not making repairs." In a low but determined voice, she added, "I'm not paying rent until the plumbing is fixed."

Mr. Underman stiffened and said, "Surely you understand that you can't live here for free."

"I will pay my rent when the pump works," Ma said, and she closed the door in Mr. Underman's face.

"You are a devil in a skirt!" he shouted through the door.

"So be it!" Ma shouted back.

We listened to his feet stomp down the stairs. "The thing I wonder," Ma said slowly, "is why that man started here with us? And two days early? Whatever his reason, it's not good."

Grandpa Jiggsy knew. He told Ma that Mr. Underman must have gotten word about the rent strike, and now he wants to find the biggest person to shake a stick at. "That's you, Clare," said Grandpa Jiggsy. "He wants to teach you a lesson the others will learn from." He put his large hand over Ma's. "Whatever you've started, we'll finish."

Later

As I left for school, Mrs. DePalma was going from door to door, saying, "Did you hear Clare Reardon? She gave it to Mr. Underman good! He's afraid of her! You should have seen how fast he ran down the stairs." The word traveled from flat to flat. The hallways filled with cheers.

By the time I got home from school, the tenants were calling Ma the new Joan of Arc. They have banded together and have promised not to pay their rent until the repairs are made.

It is cold outside, but the sun is strong. Sheets and blankets, shirts and pants flutter like victory banners from windows, fire escapes, and clotheslines stretched across the alley.

Tuesday, February 28, 1899

Again Mr. Underman came by to collect the rent. Again Ma refused to pay until the pump is fixed. Their voices rose loudly in the hall. As he left, he shouted, "Get a good night's sleep because it's the last night you'll spend here."

Wednesday, March 1, 1899

Just as I was finishing up breakfast and Ma was mashing up bread and milk for Winnie and Annie, we heard hob-nailed boots tramping up our stairs.

The tread swelled in the stairwell. Grandpa Jiggsy's grip tightened on his butter knife. I held my breath and willed the boots to round the staircase and continue on to the fifth floor, but they didn't. They stopped outside our door. Then came a loud knock.

Grandpa Jiggsy knocked over his chair as he stood to answer the door, but Ma put Winnie in his lap and told him to sit. She said it was her fight. She straightened her shoulders, took a deep breath, and opened the door.

There stood Mr. Underman, the city marshal, and six policemen. The city marshal unfolded a paper and read from it. "Mrs. John Reardon," he said, "I hereby evict you for nonpayment of rent."

Two angry red spots popped out on Ma's cheeks. She argued and pointed to the buckets next to the stove and told him how the water pump was blocked and how she had to search for water in the streets each morning.

"Sorry, lady," said the city marshal. "But I've got orders." He nodded to the policemen in that way that says get to it.

Terrified at the strange men, Annie clutched Ma's skirt

and cried. That started Winnie to bawl at the top of her lungs. I picked Winnie up and she buried her face in my shoulder.

Grandpa Jiggsy said to Mr. Underman, "In Ireland we knew how to take care of landlords like you."

Mr. Underman stiffened. A policeman stepped between them, one hand on his nightstick. It's not like my grandfather to retreat, but he grabbed his hat and stormed out.

The marshal nodded again at the policemen to get busy. Piece by piece, they carried all of our household goods downstairs: our bedding; our clothing; our kitchen table with its wobbly legs; four chairs; two three-legged stools; pots, pans, and crockery; our teakettle, still hot and spouting steam. They heaped everything on the sidewalk.

When a policeman reached for the morning glory plate on the shelf above the stove, Ma hollered, "No!" and she snatched the plate away from him.

Later

As long as I live, I will never forget how much I hate the men who evicted us.

I will never forget how shameful it feels to see all that

we own carried downstairs and heaped like garbage on the sidewalk.

I will never forget how our neighbors peered from behind their window curtains and how Mr. Underman shook his fist and shouted up at them, telling them to take a good look and learn a lesson. "If I catch anyone going through my building again, working up my tenants against me, they'll be sorry," he said.

I will never forget how Mrs. Sanko came outside and how she did not look us in the eye as she placed a saucer on the sidewalk. She mumbled a prayer and dropped a penny into it. Two men gave pennies and prayers. So did an old woman with a basket, a young mother with two small boys, and our tenement neighbors. But no one dared to look at us. No one dared to take us in. They all feared Mr. Underman.

I will never forget how the cowards paid their rent. How Mrs. DePalma came to Ma, crying, saying that her husband forbade her to make a fuss. He did not want the trouble of an eviction and would beat her if she disobeyed.

I will never forget how Ma hugged her and told her she understood and how Mrs. DePalma needed to take care of herself for the sake of her children. My mother has the forgiveness of a saint.

I will never forget how Ma held her head high like a queen, all the while clutching the morning glory plate. As each new penny clinked in the dish, the anger inside me mounted. My mother is not a beggar! I wanted to shout. We are not beggars!

Friday, March 3, 1899

Yesterday, when Winnie and Annie started to fuss from hunger and cold, Ma took a penny from the saucer and sent me to buy bananas.

I came back with four black-speckled ones. I offered one to Ma, but she shook her head no and told me to eat two. Ma peeled one and fed bits to the girls. I told Ma not to worry, that I'll sell newspapers morning and night, if I have to. But Ma said that everything will be all right, that we have our savings. We'll use some for a new flat, and she'll take in more shirts. "God never closes a door without opening a window," said Ma.

Someone shouted, "Hallo, Clare!" and we saw Grandpa Jiggsy, steaming toward us. "I found us a new flat," he said. "On Broome Street."

I scooped up the pennies and counted enough to rent a wagon from the livery stable. Before the factory whistles blew at six o'clock, we were settled into our new flat at 257 Broome Street. Ma sent me to meet Maggie and Pop on their way home from work.

At first Pop and Maggie were upset, but once they saw our new flat, they were so pleased that you'd think the move to Broome Street was their idea. Ma fussed about the rent money. Our new flat costs sixteen dollars a month, four dollars more than Mott Street.

Pop says it's a respectable flat for a man who intends to be a boss someday. I say good riddance to Mott Street and to every cowardly tenant who lives there.

Saturday, March 4, 1899

Last night Grandpa Jiggsy stayed out late and this morning his hands were bruised.

Sunday, March 5, 1899

In many ways our new flat feels strangely the same as our old one. The building is another junk heap of lumber and brick. The dark hallways smell like cooked cabbage and bootblack. The walls are dirty and dust-stained. Ma soldiers buckets, mops, and brooms and deals mighty blows to dust and dirt demons that cross enemy lines.

For sixteen dollars we have four rooms, a gas stove that hisses and sputters, and gaslights that Pop forgets to dim at night. Ma worries about the four dollars extra rent money and the cost of gas. She is determined to replace every cent of our savings.

But it's home. The rooms are filled with our family. The parlor is filled with our furniture, trunks, and boxes. And the morning glory plate sits on its shelf above the stove.

We have working pipes that bring water right to the kitchen sink. Each floor has four flats and two water closets with flush toilets. Maggie likes the *facilities*, as she calls them. My sister doesn't say *johnny closet* anymore. Now she says *facilities* and *water closet*.

I don't know what the family across the hall eats, but nobody wants to use the *facilities* after they do.

Tuesday, March 7, 1899

Ma saw Mr. Underman yesterday. He has a colorful shiner, and a bandage on his chin. When he saw Ma, he crossed to the other side of the street.

Thursday, March 9, 1899

More snow. Last night I sold twenty-three papers. As Ma cut up the leftover *Journals*, she read an article about a fire that broke out in a cap factory on Bleecker Street. No one was hurt. The girls were rescued by a quick-thinking cop and brave passersby.

News like that makes Ma worry about Maggie, who works on the top floor of the pants factory. Her factory is a firetrap, with its rickety stairs and sagging floors. The floors are littered with half-finished garments and fabric scraps and oil-soaked rags, which would burn easily. Some days, the bosses bolt the doors shut to prevent the girls from taking too many bathroom breaks.

Ma says that the girls need a union, but Maggie does not have Ma's fire. It seems funny that Ma and Maggie look so much alike but they act opposite.

Saturday, March 11, 1899

Tonight Pop brought home a man named Mr. Carmody. He wore a round derby hat perched carelessly on the back of his head, a gentleman's suit, a clean white-collared shirt and bow tie, and shiny shoes. He was about Pop's age, but he carried himself with an air of importance.

Mr. Carmody's eyes swept over our flat, taking in our furniture, our numerous boxes and trunks stacked tidily in the parlor corners, our yellowed curtains, the faded flowers in our small carpet, and our mantel with its morning glory plate.

Pop made a quick round of introductions. Mr. Carmody is a ward politician from Tammany Hall, headquarters of the most powerful political bosses in New York City. He is a man with pull, as Pop would say.

Pop asked Ma to make tea and gestured for Mr. Carmody to take a seat in our parlor. Ma didn't say a word, but she banged the teakettle on the stove. The teacups rattled as she set them down hard on the table. She doesn't like the ward politicians and their committeemen. She doesn't trust men who go around telling other men how to vote in return for favors.

But Ma did as Pop asked. She made the tea and even nudged the sugar bowl toward Mr. Carmody. Her eyes widened as he shoveled two heaping spoonfuls into his cup. Pop reached for the sugar, but Ma cleared her throat, reminding Pop that it is still Lent.

Mr. Carmody sipped his tea loudly and brought up the subject of the Irish Brotherhood Benevolent Association. He told Pop that the association meets twice a month. He said the dues cost one dollar a month and that all members must promise to vote Democrat in all the city elections.

Ma interrupted Mr. Carmody and informed him that Pop already votes Democrat. And he votes for free, without paying dues.

Mr. Carmody thought that over. Then he told Ma that a man like Pop would benefit greatly because the association members are like brothers. They are pledged to help one another in a business way.

Ma wanted to know what a "business way" meant. She wanted to know if it is a union, but Mr. Carmody said no, that the association is an organization of like-minded men. Association members help a brother find work or a better position to improve himself. He nudged Pop with an air of familiarity and said it is good for men like Pop to mix with men who can help him succeed. He called Pop "a man of considerable talent."

Pop beamed. I knew he was thinking about how much he wants to be a boss.

Encouraged by Pop's enthusiasm, Mr. Carmody leaned forward and added that if a member dies, his widow gets one hundred dollars for funeral expenses. That's enough money for a burial, a headstone, and a little left over for the family. If a member becomes sick, he receives eight dollars each week for two months and a visit from all his brothers.

"A visit from all the brothers?" said Ma. "In this small flat? Am I supposed to wait on them and serve them tea?"

Mr. Carmody didn't know the answer to that question. He said in a cheerful voice, "Perhaps you won't always live here, Mrs. Reardon. It's easy to see that your husband is a man with a future."

Pop liked hearing that. When Mr. Carmody finished his tea, Pop promised to think about the membership and to let him know his decision. Mr. Carmody picked up his hat and said good night.

Pop closed the door behind Mr. Carmody and then said, "What do you think, Clare?"

Ma weighed her words carefully. "I think I don't like the idea of paying one whole dollar each month."

Pop said, "What's a dollar, Clare? I could get hit by a streetcar tomorrow and you would wish you had paid the dollar."

"I would wish you'd been more careful, that's what I'd wish," said Ma.

Pop loves Ma, but sometimes she gives him a headache.

Monday, March 13, 1899

A new girl came to school. Bootsie Weber has long hair the color of ladybugs and legs so thin that her socks won't stay up. She is the prettiest girl I've ever seen. I guess I was staring because Mr. Drinker crashed his pointer on my desk and told me to get my head out of the clouds.

Friday, March 17, 1899

Ma says that school teaches us about the holidays poor people can't afford to celebrate, holidays like Thanksgiving and Christmas. But it doesn't teach us about the real holidays, like St. Patrick's Day, when you can watch a parade for free. So Ma says it's up to us to teach ourselves, and it's the one day I can skip and she doesn't say a word.

Ma gave me a green ribbon to tie to my coat button. The fellas and I stole rides on streetcars and rode up to Fifth Avenue and Forty-second Street, where the parade started. More than ten thousand men marched! The 69th Regiment led the parade, followed by the First Irish Volunteers, and forty-eight divisions of the Ancient Order of Hibernians. My ears filled with drums and bagpipes.

Around two-thirty, someone shouted that the Windsor Hotel was on fire. Thousands of people ran over to Forty-seventh Street. By the time we got there, the streets were jammed with onlookers, and the hotel was ablaze with flames. We watched in horror as men and women stood in the hotel windows and leaped to their death. Others fell back from the windows into the burning building. I think it must be the worst thing in the world to be burned alive.

Saturday, March 18, 1899

Tonight's *Journal* screamed about the Windsor Hotel fire. The headline says eighty-two people were killed or are missing and many injured. The entire front page was taken up with photographs that show the hotel five minutes before its walls fell and five minutes after. The dead include many wealthy and important guests, including the daughter of the hotel owner.

Racetrack sold over two hundred papers. I sold one hundred and twenty-five. When I got home, I gave Ma every cent, even my tips. It made me sick to think about how many papers a disaster like the Windsor Hotel fire helped me to sell.

Monday, March 20, 1899

Today is the first day of spring. Grandpa Jiggsy says that the first day of spring and the first spring day are a month apart.

In the Bowery, we know it's spring when the peddlers come out of winter hibernation and fill the streets with their cries. From their two-wheeled pushcarts, they hawk everything from fruits to vegetables to chestnuts to flowers, and even dry goods like thread and ribbons.

Thursday, March 23, 1899

Each time Mr. Drinker's pointer crashes, Bootsie shrinks like a mouse. I want to tell Bootsie that Mr. Drinker would never hit her. Her copybook is perfection, her handwriting the neatest in the class, her lessons learned by heart. I want to tell Bootsie that teachers like Mr. Drinker pick on fellas like Jimmy because it keeps them in practice for the targets they're really after. Fellas like Racetrack.

Sunday, March 26, 1899

Palm Sunday. Ma asked Pop to go to Mass, but he said no. He said the rich man is rich because he only asks God for favors every great while. But the poor man is poor because he always nags God for one thing or another.

Tuesday, March 28, 1899

Tonight Pop announced that our bad luck has changed to good luck.

If it weren't for the eviction, Pop said, he never would have had a drink in O'Brien's Saloon next to our tenement. If it weren't for the saloon, he says, he never would have met such a fine gentleman as Mr. Carmody. And if it weren't for Mr. Carmody, Pop would never have joined the Irish Brotherhood.

"You joined the Brotherhood?" said Ma.

"That's not the point," said Pop.

I could tell that Ma thought it was the point.

Pop told Ma how he attended his first Brotherhood meeting in the back room of the Hibernian Hall on Prince Street. There Mr. Carmody introduced Pop to a man named Mr. Hoban, who deals in real estate. He told Pop that his business is booming because people with money are moving out of Manhattan to the Bronx, Brooklyn, and other growing sections of New York City. He calls the new areas the suburbs.

Mr. Hoban told Pop that he needed a man to paint the houses that he builds. He said that an ambitious man could make money and a name for himself.

"And do you know who that ambitious man is, Clare?" said Pop.

"Who?" said Ma.

Pop seemed annoyed that Ma didn't guess. "Me," he said, jabbing himself in the chest with his thumb.

Ma seemed shocked. "You?"

"I start next week," said Pop. "I am in the painting business. What do you think about that?"

"What do you know about painting houses?" said Ma.

"What is there to know?" said Pop. "You mix the linseed oil and turpentine with the paint powder. You stick in your brush, and you paint the house."

"You will need paint and other supplies like brushes and ladders and scaffolding," said Ma. "Where will you get the money to buy these things?"

Pop had already thought about that. He reached into the kitchen cupboard and pulled out the savings jar. "It takes money to make money," he said. "Our savings will help me buy the things I need and hire a few workers."

The color drained from Ma's face.

"Our bad luck has changed to good luck," said Pop. He grabbed Ma and danced her around the kitchen.

I can't help thinking about something Ma always says. She says if something sounds too good to be true, it probably is.

Sunday, April 2, 1899

I thought Ma was going to keel over when Pop came out of the bedroom wearing his white shirt and bow tie. Pop said, "Are you ready?" and Ma said, "For what?" and he said, "For Mass. It's Easter, isn't it?" Ma looked so happy that we would go to church as a family that I thought she was going to melt right down and cry.

Friday, April 7, 1899

It's only been one week since Pop became a painter boss and already he is a new man. In the morning, Ma doesn't soldier him out of bed. He leaps up, splashes cold water onto his face, and goes off whistling to work. He is a man in a hurry.

It is only one week, but Pop has a contract to paint five houses in Borough Park, a growing section of Brooklyn, and Mr. Hoban has promised more. As soon as Pop signed the contract, he withdrew fifty dollars from our savings account at the Bowery Savings Bank. "It takes money to make money," Pop told Ma again.

It is only one week, but our parlor is cluttered with brushes, two ladders, and cans of paint, varnish, turpentine, and linseed oil.

It is only one week, but Pop has hired four painters to help him. The men are Italian and don't speak very much English. Pop explained to Ma that they were the cheapest hands he could find. Grandpa Jiggsy is also going to work for Pop.

It is only one week, but Pop no longer walks home at the end of each day. He struts and swings his shoulders with an air of importance.

It is only one week, but at night Pop talks about our someday house.

Monday, April 17, 1899

It's the rush season in the pants factory where Maggie works. When Maggie comes home, she is so pale and tired that she eats a bite of supper, washes her blouse for the next day, has a good cry, and then goes right to bed.

Today Maggie was fined an hour's wages — ten cents — for taking too long in the bathroom. Her boss has also made a new rule: The girls aren't allowed to sing or talk as they work.

Ma told Maggie that the girls need a union, but Pop said he doesn't believe in unions. He believes in associations. Pop said that each man in America should be allowed to make his own fortune, and that's exactly what he intends to do. "If a man works hard and owns his own business, why should his workers tell him how to run his business?" says Pop. "If my workers don't like working for me, then let them get jobs elsewhere."

Ma reminded Pop that the rich get rich on the backs of the poor. She said all the poor have is their own strength, but Pop didn't listen. "Don't speak ill of the rich," he told Ma. "The poor aren't hiring."

Friday, April 21, 1899

Tonight after I sold my newspapers, I stopped at O'Brien's Saloon to get Pop for dinner. Since he has joined the Brotherhood, he doesn't sit at the bar anymore. He sits in a rear room with his new brothers. The long, narrow room is lit with gas lamps that hang like white balloons from the ceiling, and is filled with smoke and talk. It smells of stale beer and too many breaths.

When Pop saw me, he grinned wide and introduced me to everyone. Then he said, "This is my son, Finn, who will someday be president of the United States."

The brothers laughed and shook my hand and said, friendly-like, "Hello, Mr. President."

I wanted to tell Pop that somebody else is going to

have to be president of the United States. As soon as I turn fourteen, I am through with school. But I didn't. Instead, I told Pop it's time for dinner.

Thursday, May 4, 1899

Sold fifty papers. Made four cents in tips. Shouted about a factory girl who was struck by lightning and lived to tell about it. She was carrying an umbrella and standing in a puddle at the time. The bolt passed right through her body, 250,000 volts' worth. It blistered her nose and chin, reduced her dress to ashes, and ripped off her right shoe.

Friday, May 5, 1899

The New Amsterdam Gas Company sent a man to knock on all the doors in the tenements on our Broome Street block. He told the families that his company will charge lower prices for the manufactured gas that lights our lamps and stoves. "Just sign here," he said, "and we will change the meters."

Pop met with the other tenants in the back of the saloon on the ground floor at No. 259 to discuss the change. The small room was hot and packed tightly with men. Soon the meeting turned from a discussion about the gas company to an argument about the gas plants and the city.

A peddler argued that the city should take over the gas plants so that the prices will be fixed and everyone, rich and poor, will pay the same amount for gas.

Pop doesn't agree. He doesn't believe the government should interfere with private businesses. "Why should the city own the gas plants?" said Pop. "What if the city decided it wanted to own your pushcart?"

"Then every pushcart man would make the same amount of money," said the peddler. "I wouldn't have to worry about how many people are hungry for bananas."

A tailor who lives in the tenement next to ours agreed, saying, "The gas companies charge too much. If the prices were fixed, we would all pay the same."

"Do you want the government telling you how much to charge for a new suit?" asked Pop.

"Not everyone needs a new suit," said the tailor. "But we all need gas."

"In America, everyone has a right to make his own fortune," said Pop. "Even the rich."

The two Russian brothers who mend opera glasses sided with Pop. The brothers said that if the government owns the gas plants, then only the rich parts of the city would get gas.

And so the argument went. Later, Pop recounted the argument to Ma, word for word. "What do you think, Clare?" said Pop.

Ma thought it over. I knew she was thinking about Pop, how he likes to read my leftover *Journals* late into the night and how he forgets to turn down the gas lamp, no matter how often she scolds. "If we're going to waste gas," she said, "at least we will pay less for it."

With a great flourish, Pop signed his name to the papers.

Tuesday, May 9, 1899

The past few days, the New Amsterdam Gas Company workmen have been clanging around our tenement. They are changing the gas pipe connections in every tenement on our street. Our hallways always smell sour, but lately there's been an oily smell beneath the sour one.

After school, I dropped my books on the kitchen chair. Ma was standing at the table, peeling potatoes. "Don't leave your books there," she said. "The Good Lord gave you two hands, one to pick up what the other puts down."

The clanging echoed through our flat. Ma dropped the vegetables into a blackened soup pot on the stove. The gas flame leaped blue and yellow beneath the pot. "I wish the workmen would finish already," said Ma. "Their clanging gives me a headache. I've told them so, but nobody listens to women, especially poor ones."

Wednesday, May 10, 1899

Something terrible has happened. It's dark and I am sitting on our fire escape, writing by the light of a kerosene lamp. Ma won't turn on the gaslight because she fears another explosion. Smoke lingers in the air.

Around six-thirty, I had sold all but two papers and decided to call it a night. I was hungry and tired and had arithmetic homework to finish.

The streets overflowed with workers heading home to their tenements. I dashed past peddlers yelling, "Apples! Apples! Fine apples!" or, "Cabbage! Cabbage! Fine cabbage!" as they trundled their pushcarts up Division Street. I weaved between housewives carrying buckets, baskets, and armfuls of wood. I dodged little kids playing on the sidewalk.

I turned north onto Allen Street. Overhead on the elevated railroad, the El train rattled and coughed black smoke and rained down cinders. As I crossed Hester Street, I heard a rumble, and the ground swelled beneath my feet. At first I dismissed the rumble as another train, but then black smoke rose like a thundercloud over my block.

I ran. As I turned the corner onto Broome Street, smoke stung my eyes. It was pouring from the windows of the tenement at No. 261, just two buildings down from ours. The street was choked with people, yelling and crying, "Fire!" Some carried babies and pulled small children by the arms. Others carried candlesticks, dishes, clocks, trunks, anything at all they could salvage.

Frantic, I searched for Ma and the girls. Bells clanged, and men shouted to clear the streets, to make way for the fire wagons. The wagons roared down the street, pulled by teams of wild-eyed horses. Sparks flew as the horses' hooves struck the pavement.

Firemen leaped off the wagons and tugged at great coils of hose. Flames swept out of the windows. Something crashed and I heard broken glass. "Get back! Get back!" the men yelled. They attached the hoses to the street hydrants. More shouts, then fountains of water gushed upward.

I found Ma and the girls outside our building. Annie tugged at my pant leg. I picked her up. Ma held Winnie and something bundled in her cloak. I knew without asking that it was her blue-flowered plate.

"You okay?" I asked. Ma pushed her dark hair back behind her ear. Dirt streaked her cheek. She nodded. Other than smoke, more falling-down ceiling plaster, and another spidery crack in our kitchen wall, we are okay.

Thursday, May 11, 1899

I am so tired that it is hard to concentrate in school. It was nearly midnight when the last fire wagon rolled back to the station last night and the commotion died down.

On the fire escapes above and below me, people talked in hushed voices about the explosion. A smoker had tossed a lit cigar to the ground, causing leaking gas to explode. The explosion knocked down passersby, tore holes in the floor and walls, and blew out the glass saloon windows.

In whispers and prayers, the tenants talked about the little Lipschitz girl, who was skipping rope when a piece of flying glass from the saloon cut her right eye. It looks as though she might lose the eye. "It could have been any one of our children," a woman said in a hushed voice.

Friday, May 12, 1899

A fire always makes a big headline with plenty of exclamation points. I splurged on one hundred *Journals*, double my usual Thursday number. I wanted to tell everyone about the New Amsterdam Gas Company and the sorrow it caused the people on my block.

I looked all over the sheets for the story about the explosion. Nothing. Not one word. Was it because no one important had been hurt?

Infuriated, I decided that if the *Journal* wouldn't tell the story, I would. I held up a paper and shouted, "Extra! Extra! Read all about it! Careless Workmen Cause Explosion!" as several gents approached. They each bought a paper.

I worked my corner, hollering my head off. More gents and several ladies pressed pennies into my hand and bought copies. A gent wearing a brown fedora handed me a nickel and didn't wait for his change. The coins felt light in my pocket as I counted my papers. Only nineteen more to sell.

Suddenly, a hand gripped my shoulder. I turned to see the gent wearing the brown fedora who had given me the nickel. Thinking he had returned for his change, I said, "Sorry, sir," and fumbled in my pocket for his pennies.

But he didn't want change. He held up the *Journal* and said sternly, "What are you pulling, kid? There's nothing in this newspaper about an explosion. You can find yourself in trouble making up lies like that."

It wasn't a lie and I told him so. I told him I ought to know because the explosion happened on my street. His eyes narrowed the way Ma's eyes do when she listens to one of Racetrack's stories. "Can you prove it?" he asked.

"Sure can," I said. And I told him to ask anyone who lives on my block and he'll hear how the New Amsterdam Gas Company talked all the Broome Street tenants into changing gas companies, and how the gas company ignored the tenants' complaints when they said they smelled gas.

Interest flickered across the gent's face. He took out a small black notebook and pencil stub from his vest pocket. He flipped open the notebook and told me to start from the beginning and tell him everything I knew. As I talked, he scribbled down notes. He told me I had an eye for detail. Then he asked my name.

"Finn," I said, "Finn Reardon." He wrote that down, too. He snapped his notebook shut and slipped it into his vest pocket. Then he handed me a quarter and bought the rest of my papers, all nineteen of them! I fished for his change, but he said, "Keep it."

"Thanks for the tip!" I said.

"Ditto," he said. With long strides, he headed back toward the newspaper office on Park Row.

Now I can't stop thinking about that gent's little black notebook and how he had scribbled down all I said, including my name. In all my thirteen years, it's never good news when a grown-up writes down your name. I don't believe in looking for trouble, and now I wonder what sort of trouble is looking for me.

Saturday, May 13, 1899

Mr. Brown Fedora found me at my corner last night. He handed me a folded newspaper and told me to take a look. It was Thursday night's final edition of the *Journal*.

Right there on the front page, this headline leaped out at me: "A Tenement Explosion. Injuries Result from Carelessness of Workmen Changing Gas Connections." No bold type and no exclamation points, but the article told all about the gas company's carelessness.

I whistled and he told me again that I have an eye for detail. The sort of eye that reporters have. Hearing those words made my head swell two sizes.

It turns out that Mr. Brown Fedora is Mr. Jack Watkins, a freelance reporter. He's tall with clear gray eyes that take in everything. He told me he gets paid by the space, anywhere from three to six dollars a column. If his story makes the front page, he gets paid a bonus.

I whistled again. A bonus! Imagine that! I told him it must feel great to be the gent who writes the news instead of the fella who shouts the news.

Mr. Watkins shook my hand and said, "It's all about words, my friend. Whether you shout them or write them, words bring about change."

He flipped me a quarter and told me if I ever have another scoop, I can leave a message for him at Murphy's Saloon near City Hall Park, where he rents an upstairs room.

Sunday, May 14, 1899

Words didn't help Ma and me wash the soot from our walls, our floor, our furniture, our beds, and our clothing. Words aren't helping the little Lipschitz girl who might lose her eye.

Ma says we're lucky that we still have a roof over our heads. The tenants from No. 261 had to leave their flats and depend on city charities or family and friends to take them in. For Ma, there's no shame in being poor, but charity makes her feel beholden to others.

Monday, May 15, 1899

The closer we get to the superintendent's examination, the more peppermints Mr. Drinker chews.

Today went like this:

Crash! we must know our grammar. "Mr. Reardon, what is a verb?" Mr. Drinker barked.

I popped to my feet and said, "Sir, a verb is a word that signifies to be, to do, or to suffer."

"Example!" demanded Mr. Drinker.

"I am, I rule, I am ruled," I told him.

"There's hope for you yet," said Mr. Drinker.

Crash! we must know how to diagram our sentences. As soon as he said the word "diagram," nearly every girl waved her hand in the air, begging to be sent to the board. The girls love to use the chalk.

Mr. Drinker picked Bootsie. "Miss Weber," he said, "diagram the following sentence: 'The school of experience teaches many useful lessons.'" He handed Bootsie a slender piece of chalk. It was a fresh piece, plucked right out of the chalk box.

With an even hand, Bootsie drew a long horizontal line, then a vertical dividing line. She wrote out the subject and predicate. Then she drew slanted lines and more horizontal lines. As she filled in the words, Mr. Drinker called out their function: article, preposition, object of the preposition, adjective, adjective, direct object.

It was a beautiful diagram. Mr. Drinker nodded in approval and told her she had a fine fist.

The blissful moment ended. Crash! the pointer came down again. We must know our spelling. He called on Rebecca Caughey and fired word after word at her.

Crash! we must know our multiplication tables. "Mr. Vaskey," he said, "recite the nineses."

Jimmy got as far as four times nine before he slipped. Mr. Drinker told him to write out the nineses twenty-five times. Jimmy reached for his copybook. "Not now," barked Mr. Drinker. "For homework."

Sometimes I wonder if Jimmy will ever learn.

Later

Jimmy had a hangdog look as we left school. "I don't know why I can't remember the nineses," said Jimmy. "I just can't."

"You've got to get tough with yourself and learn them," I said. "If you don't get tough, you get hurt." That's what Grandpa Jiggsy always tells me.

Outside, Bootsie Weber stood on the steps. "I need to talk to you," she said.

My heart nearly leaped out of my chest. I glanced over

my shoulder, sure she was talking to someone behind me. I saw no one except Jimmy.

My face grew hot. Bootsie wanted to talk to me and I couldn't put two words together. I stood there stupidly with my mouth open, trying to gather my wits.

Bootsie asked if I would hold her books. I practically snatched the books out of her hands. I nudged Jimmy as a hint to tell him to leave us alone.

Jimmy started away, but Bootsie called after him. "Jimmy, come back," she said. "I want to talk to you."

Jimmy's ears grew red. "Me?" he said, but it sounded like a squawk. Jimmy was even more shy around girls than I was.

"Jimmy," said Bootsie, "I don't want you to get into any more trouble with Mr. Drinker, so I'm going to show you how to do the nineses on your fingers."

Jimmy broke into a grin as Bootsie showed him. It's a simple trick, really, and if I hadn't felt so peevish, I might have been amazed. I kicked at a stone and sent it sailing. As I headed to Newspaper Row, I'm ashamed to admit a small part of me wished that Mr. Drinker would catch them both.

Tuesday, May 16, 1899

I was sitting in the kitchen, holding my head in my hands and feeling downhearted and sorry for myself. Maggie came home, happy and humming to herself.

Before I knew it, I was asking Maggie how a fella goes about getting a girl to notice him.

As soon as I asked, I winced inside, wondering if she'd laugh at me, but she didn't. She said that girls like a clean fella, one who knows how to wash his face and hands and comb his hair. Girls also like honesty and good manners, and girls who don't, well, it's best to leave them alone. Then Maggie said, "Give her a present."

I told her that I had no idea when Bootsie's birthday was. She said that was all the better, that girls like surprises, especially presents.

I don't know why my sister is in a good mood. Tonight she hasn't complained once that I am scribbling away while she is trying to sleep.

Thursday, May 18, 1899

I took Maggie's advice and spent a whole nickel on chocolate candy for Bootsie.

This morning I scrubbed my face and slicked back

my hair. I started out early for school, feeling so light-hearted that Ma grew suspicious. I whistled all the way down the stairs. Outside, I looked up toward our flat, and there was Ma, her face pressed against the window, making sure I was headed toward school. I waved. She waved back.

At school, I headed straight for Bootsie's desk. Just as I sneaked the chocolate candy inside, someone said, "What do you think you're doing?"

It was Rebecca Caughey. She told me to stay out of Bootsie's desk. I told her it's a free country, in case she hasn't noticed, and I can do anything I want.

"I'm telling," said Rebecca.

"See if I care," I said. "You're just jealous." Then I told Rebecca that if she's wondering why no one gave her candy, she should chase herself to a mirror and she'd see why.

The minute the words came out, I winced. It was a mean thing to say. Her eyes tightened. She huffed and spun on her heel. "Wait," I said, wanting to apologize.

As the class straggled in, I forgot about Rebecca and clowned around in the back of the room with Racetrack and the other fellas while I watched for Bootsie.

Soon Bootsie came through the doorway and headed straight to her desk. She lifted the lid and gasped. She looked around to see who her admirer was. I gave her a little wave. My insides cheered as she waved back.

Then Rebecca sailed over to Bootsie and buzzed in her ear. "A worm?" said Bootsie, making a face.

My stomach sank. "It was third grade!" I said. "And it was a small one!"

It didn't matter. Together, they wrapped up the chocolates and threw them away. Bootsie didn't look at me again all day. Rebecca has convinced her that I'm a disgusting creature.

Later

I will not think about Bootsie Weber. I will not waste another journal page on her.

Friday, May 19, 1899

The five houses are painted. Pleased with Pop's work, Mr. Hoban has given him another contract, this time ten houses.

Never have I seen Pop in a better mood. He pulled Ma away from the sink and started to sing "My Pearl Is a Bowery Girl." He danced her around the kitchen and into the parlor, never bumping the chairs or the wall.

Ma's hands pressed her hair into place, and her eyes, those morning glory eyes that rule our flat, smiled at Pop.

Saturday, May 20, 1899

We checked out our fort at Corlear's Hook Park. Our fort is a junk heap of rotted boards, but it's a place where we can roast sweet potatoes and camp out in the summer.

We spent the morning cleaning up the fort, fixing the boards, and making plans for improvements. Then we headed down to the pier to watch the boats.

The river was busy. There were big ships and little boats, pilot boats built low in the water, and huge freighters loaded with cargo. Ferries plowed through the gray water, carrying workers across the river.

In the distance, a stout tugboat heaved into view, puffing like a bulldog. Racetrack said he likes the tugboats best, which didn't surprise me. Racetrack *is* a tugboat, the way he pulls people along with him, changing their course.

We stood at the pier's edge, looking down at the swirling water twenty feet below. Suddenly, Racetrack said, "I dare you fellas to jump."

Racetrack never dares someone to do something that he wouldn't do. "You jump," I said, hoping he'd back down.

"I will," he said. He kicked off his shoes and pulled off his shirt and pants until he stood in his underwear.

Now I was stuck. I'd lose face if I didn't jump. Not with

the fellas, because they don't care who goes along and who doesn't. But I would know. I didn't want them to have one thing up on me.

I yanked my shirt over my head and dropped my pants. Mush and Grin did the same. Grin said, "Who's jumping first?"

"We all jump at once," said Racetrack.

That's when we looked at Jimmy, still completely dressed. He blinked twice. "I can't swim," he said.

Mush started to tease him about that, but Racetrack stopped him and said, "Then you're the lookout, Jimmy. You can guard our clothes."

Jimmy nodded, obviously relieved.

Racetrack whooped, and we all took off running down the dock. After all, Grandpa says it's perfectly legal to jump off a pier as long as a fella wears his underwear.

Later

The water was so cold, it took my breath away when we hit. But the sun was strong, and after we climbed out, we stretched out on the pier to dry off. Anything a fella does in the sun is fun.

Racetrack said our gang should have an initiation. Mush suggested the initiation should be to jump off the pier. We liked that idea, but Jimmy grew quiet and reminded us that he can't swim. Racetrack told him to clear his mind of "can't." That's another of Racetrack's rules. He says "can't" means you don't want to. "Just tell yourself that you *want* to learn," Racetrack told Jimmy. "We'll teach you this summer."

Jimmy nodded. That's why Racetrack is a tugboat. He pulled Jimmy right along and even convinced him that we could teach him how to swim.

Tuesday, May 23, 1899

Still not thinking about Bootsie Weber.

Tortured all day by Mr. Drinker. Thirteen more days of school before summer, and then I never have to suffer Mr. Drinker ever again.

Ma has no sympathy when I complain about Mr. Drinker, who piles on the work like there's no tomorrow. Ma says there are teachers you like and teachers you don't like and you can learn from both kinds, if you put your head to it. She expects good grades no matter what I think of Mr. Drinker and school.

Friday, May 26, 1899

It was three peppermints past one o'clock when Mr. Drinker called on Jimmy to recite the nines times tables. Jimmy stood clumsily with his head down and began to recite $0 \times 9 = 0$, $1 \times 9 = 9$, $2 \times 9 = 18$, $3 \times 9 = 27$ . . .

And then it happened. The movement was so slight that I almost missed it. But I saw it and so did Mr. Drinker. His eyes popped. Crash! he slammed his pointer onto Jimmy's desk. "Mr. Vaskey," he said. "Are you using your fingers?"

The color drained from Jimmy's face. He swallowed hard. "Yes, sir," he said.

Mr. Drinker stared hard at us, and we withered beneath his gaze. "Someone in this class does not want you to use your head," he said. "Who is it? Speak up!"

Up and down the rows, chairs creaked as everyone shifted nervously, but no one answered. I knew what Mr. Drinker would do next. He would ask each of us, one by one, who taught Jimmy. He might even test us, to see who else did the nineses on their fingers.

Bootsie's face grew terribly troubled. My stomach twisted, but I reminded myself that she had nothing but pure meanness in her. It was just a matter of time until Mr. Drinker found her out, and then she deserved whatever punishment she got.

I glanced at her again and saw that she was ready to burst out crying and confess. Suddenly, I couldn't bear the thought of Bootsie's humiliation in front of the whole class. A thought surged through me. I would take the blame. I would tell Mr. Drinker that I'd taught Jimmy, and then Bootsie would see that I am not some disgusting creature.

It's hard enough to confess to something you *did* do, let alone something you *didn't* do. I tried to raise my hand, but I couldn't. I wanted to speak out, but no words would come.

Just then, Racetrack said, "I did it. I taught Jimmy."

We stared in amazement as Racetrack walked to the front of the room. Mr. Drinker reached for his paddle from the closet door and gave two whacks to Jimmy and five to Racetrack. It was the most he's ever doled out.

Mr. Drinker thinks he has won, but he hasn't. If he read our eyes, he would see that we hailed Racetrack as a hero. At that moment, I never admired anyone more.

And I never felt more ashamed.

Thursday, June 1, 1899

Racetrack said it's time our gang had a purpose. He said every gang has a line of business, so to speak.

Jimmy said, "We should become burglars."

"What would we burgle?" said Racetrack.

"Money from banks," said Mush.

"That's robbery, not burglary," said Racetrack.

Grin said, "What's the difference?"

"You'll find out when the judge sends you to jail," said Racetrack. "Isn't that right, Finn?"

"That's right," I said, even though I don't know the difference between a burglar and a robber.

Friday, June 2, 1899

When school let out, I made up an excuse about schoolwork to the fellas and told them to go ahead to Newspaper Row without me. I needed to find out the difference between a burglar and a robber.

As soon as the room cleared out, I approached Mr. Drinker. He was sitting behind his desk, reading our latest compositions. I cleared my throat. He looked up, and I asked if I could borrow his dictionary.

He warned me that I had better not want to look up any *immoral* words. I assured him I didn't.

He narrowed his eyes in suspicion, and then he looked pleased. "Ah, yes," he said. "You're preparing for the superintendent's examination." And Mr. Drinker did something I have never seen before. He smiled.

Mr. Drinker got up and went over to his closet. As he swung open the door, the wooden paddle thumped lightly and swayed on its hook. I had a sudden flash of Jimmy and Racetrack, and I felt a spark of hatred for that paddle.

Mr. Drinker pulled out a thick dictionary from the middle shelf. He handed it to me with a stern look to let me know he was keeping an eye on me. I carried the dictionary back to my desk.

Now, the thing about the dictionary is that it never just tells you what a word means. It sends you hunting from word to word. I looked up *burglar*, and it told me that a burglar is someone who commits burglary. I looked up *burglary*, and it told me that burglary is the act of breaking and entering a dwelling to commit a felony. So I looked up *felony*, and it told me that a felony is a crime for which the punishment by federal law may be death or imprisonment for more than one year.

Death or imprisonment! Ma would kill me first!

Then I needed to know about robbers, so I looked up the word and it told me what I already know: A *robber* is a person who robs. I looked up *rob*, and it said to rob is to engage in *robbery* or to take something away by violence or threat. I looked up *robbery*, and it means the act or practice of robbing. I closed the dictionary. I don't want to be a burglar *or* a robber.

Just then Mr. Drinker picked up his head, and with genuine regret he told me it was getting late and I'd best be getting home. He tipped his head toward his closet and told me to put the dictionary away. Then he bent over our compositions.

I didn't look at the paddle as I opened the closet door and slid the dictionary into its place between the other books. But I did look to see the sorts of things that Mr. Drinker kept in his closet. He had a poetry book, a Bible, three boxes of new chalk, peppermints, and a toothbrush with the bristles worn down.

As I started to close the closet door, the paddle thumped lightly, and an idea flashed in my head. I looked at Mr. Drinker, still bent over our work. Quietly, I lifted the paddle from its hook and slipped it inside my shirt and pants.

"Good night, Mr. Drinker," I said, closing the closet door.

"Good night, Mr. Reardon," he said, never looking up.

It's risky for a fella to walk with a paddle stuck down his pants, and a bit tricky. I wanted to run, but I willed myself to walk from the classroom. I continued stiffly down the hall, straining my ears, expecting Mr. Drinker to call after me. He didn't.

Outside, I picked up my pace. At the end of the block, I turned onto Delancey Street. The school no longer in sight, I stopped and took out the paddle. My legs trembled inside my pants as I held it in my hand.

Hardly believing what I'd done, I carried it home and stowed it behind the boxes in the parlor.

Later

It's midnight and I cannot sleep. This is the most foolish stunt I have ever pulled. Surely Mr. Drinker will discover his missing paddle. Surely he will put two and two together and know that I have taken it.

Sunday, June 4, 1899

My conscience has given me no peace since I stole that paddle. I tossed around all night and had terrible dreams. I dreamed that Mr. Drinker was leading me off to the penitentiary in chains.

At breakfast Ma asked if something was troubling me.

She said I've been pitching around and talking in my sleep. She wanted to know if I had something to tell her.

That rattled my nerves. A burglar doesn't want to hear that he talks in his sleep. "What did I say?" I asked cautiously. She said she heard me call out Mr. Drinker's name over and over.

Mr. Drinker's face and his paddle went swimming before me. My hand shook so that I spilled my tea. I gulped and said, "Anything more?" She said no, that his name was all she could make out.

I wanted to confess to Ma right then and there. But when a fella's gone and done the worst thing he has ever done in his entire life, there's a part of him that doesn't want to see the heartbreak it would cause. He especially doesn't want to tell his mother that she has a common crook living beneath her roof.

Monday, June 5, 1899

It was ninety-one degrees today and we sat and sweated as we took the city superintendent's sixth-grade examination. Everyone, that is, except Racetrack, who didn't show up. Lucky dog.

I don't like tests, but today I felt grateful because it kept my head too busy to think about the paddle. We did arithmetic the first hour, and geography and history the second hour. The third hour was spent on grammar, diagramming sentences, composition, and a huge spelling test. I finished and turned in my examination. My hand is so sore that I can't bear to write another word in this journal.

Later

It was two-thirty and the superintendent was collecting our examinations when Mr. Drinker caught Grin Boyle in some foolishness. I did not see what Grin did. The next thing I knew, Mr. Drinker pounced on Grin and jerked him out of his seat and to the front of the room.

Grin stood, meek and resigned, as Mr. Drinker yanked open his closet door. The room filled with gasps as everyone saw the paddle was gone.

Mr. Drinker looked as though someone had struck him over the head. He stared at the empty hook. Then he searched from one shelf to the other.

Clearly flustered, Mr. Drinker straightened and faced us. He said, "There's something —" then stopped. He looked at the superintendent, then us, reconsidered his words, and started again, "Someone has clearly —" Once more, he stopped. He cleared his throat, adjusted his collar, and tried again. "A certain item of mine —"

Mr. Drinker knew that he had a dilemma. If he admitted that someone had stolen his paddle, the superintendent might question his ability to maintain discipline over his students. But if Mr. Drinker didn't seek out the culprit, he would lose the upper hand.

His eyes flitted toward me for a second, then roved until they settled on Racetrack's empty seat. His eyes narrowed, and I could feel Mr. Drinker ticking off Racetrack's absences and then dismiss him as a suspect. He scanned the room for another culprit.

Finding none, Mr. Drinker gripped Grin's shoulder and gave him a good scolding about foolishness and lectured him on the importance of an education and the value of self-discipline. He told us that knowledge has saved many a man and that he hoped we would carry our lessons into the world and make something out of ourselves. Then he told Grin to sit down.

It was a beautiful speech, and the city superintendent looked pleased. Smiling broadly, he pumped Mr. Drinker's hand vigorously, saying he was glad to see that Mr. Drinker was a progressive teacher, one who utilized the power of words and persuasion over the power of the paddle. "A paddle cannot beat out stupidity and poverty," said the superintendent. "Only knowledge can." Then he told our class that Mr. Drinker was a fine teacher and surely we are destined for seventh grade next year. He tucked our examinations under his arm and he left.

Mr. Drinker sat, slumped behind his desk. He glanced from his closet to us, from us to his closet. The minutes ticked by slowly until the clock struck three. Mr. Drinker absently dismissed us with a wave of his hand.

Wednesday, June 7, 1899

Our final examination is over, and that should mean that school is over, but no, we still have to finish the week. Mr. Drinker intends to torture us with reading, writing, and arithmetic right up until the very last second of the last minute of the last hour of the last day of the school year.

We sweated and summed and recited until three o'clock. Then he loaded us with homework and dismissed us. As I passed his desk, he picked up his head and said, "Mr. Reardon, give this to your mother." He handed me a sealed envelope.

It took the knees right out from under me as it was a note. A note to Ma.

Later

I could not look Ma in the eye as I handed her the note. Ma read it, and it turns out that Mr. Drinker wants to see her tomorrow at three o'clock. He wants to talk to her about my future.

Ma worried out loud that she had no one to mind Annie and Winnie. I tried to keep the quaver out of my voice as I told Ma that it was all right, that Mr. Drinker would understand if she could not come to school, but she said no, that it was good for teachers and parents to put their heads together over a boy's future.

Thursday, June 8, 1899

Thunderstorms all last night. The air cooled for an hour or two, then blistering heat returned. The heat has killed twenty-two people in New York City, mostly babies and the elderly.

All day, I sweated and prayed that Ma would forget about Mr. Drinker's note and their appointment. But no, there Ma stood at three o'clock sharp in the hallway with Winnie and Annie. It's not the sight a fella wants to see when he's coming out of school.

It was blazing hot, but Ma wore a freshly ironed white

blouse and her black skirt. Her blouse was worn thin at the elbows, but she had dressed it up with the cameo brooch that had belonged to her mother. Ma had borrowed a black handbag from someone. She fiddled with the clasp, opening and closing it, click click click.

Mr. Drinker came to the door and said, "Thank you for coming, Mrs. Reardon."

Ma handed Winnie to me. She told them to be good girls while she visited with the nice man. Then she whisked inside, closing the door behind her.

Now Ma and Mr. Drinker are sitting in there, buzzing about me. I feel like a prisoner awaiting his sentence. The clock is ticking. Winnie has fallen asleep in my lap, and Annie has squeezed herself next to me. She is half asleep, sucking her thumb as she leans against my shoulder. Both girls smell like pee.

Later

When the classroom door creaked opened and Ma emerged at last, her cheeks were wet with tears and she was swallowing hard.

Mr. Drinker's stiff manner had disappeared. He handed Ma his handkerchief. She wiped her eyes, then blew her nose hard and handed the handkerchief back. Mr. Drinker said that was all right, Ma could keep it. She started to tuck it in her sleeve. Remembering the handbag, she stuck it inside instead.

Winnie woke up, smiled at Mr. Drinker, and then buried her face shyly in my neck. Mr. Drinker pulled out two peppermints from his pocket and gave one to each of the girls. Annie smacked loudly on her peppermint. "Nice man," she said. Mr. Drinker laughed out loud and patted her on the head.

Ma didn't say a word all the way home, and my insides twisted in agony. When we reached our flat, Ma put on the kettle to boil. She poured herself a cup of tea and sat, holding her teacup in both hands. A tear fell down her cheek. She wiped it away.

I couldn't take my eyes off the boxes stacked in the parlor. I couldn't stop thinking about the paddle hidden there. Unable to stand the suffering any longer, I blurted, "Ma, I know what Mr. Drinker told you!"

Ma looked over her teacup at me and said, "You do?"

I nodded, unable to speak.

"Then you know how proud I am of you," she said.

And she told me how Mr. Drinker said most of my classmates are going to the dogs, but I'm the sort of young man to stay after school, using his dictionary to prepare for the examination. He told her that I had passed with flying colors, the highest marks in the class. He said that any boy with my grades and my love of words has a future ahead of him, if he stays on the straight and narrow.

Then Ma said Mr. Drinker told her that I should set my sights high. She told him that I would be the first in our family to finish grammar school and go on to high school. But no, that wasn't good enough for Mr. Drinker. He told Ma that I have what it takes to go beyond high school. I should set my sights on college.

I looked at Ma and saw nothing but pride and hope in her eyes and knew I'd heard the word that made Ma cry. College.

Friday, June 9, 1899

It's late and Ma thinks I'm in bed. I have turned up the gaslight just enough to scribble a few words.

I have felt troubled and sick to my stomach ever since I pulled that foolish stunt and stole the paddle.

Last night I got it in my head that I could return the paddle before school this morning. Perhaps the fellas would help me sneak it back into the school. Burglary was breaking and entering and stealing something, not putting something back.

My conscience began to feel less troubled, and for the

first time in days, my stomach stopped jumping. I had done something wrong. Now I would make it right. So this morning I wrapped up the paddle in my jacket and carried it down to Newspaper Row.

I found Racetrack and told him that I needed his help. I showed him the paddle.

"That's Mr. Drinker's paddle!" said Racetrack. Then he hollered to the others. "Look!"

Jimmy's mouth dropped open. Mush clapped me on the back and said, "That's the best stunt ever."

Grin said, "Congratulations, pal!"

The fellas cheered and whistled. Something inside my head swelled, and I puffed up with importance.

Racetrack took the paddle from me. He took out a pocketknife. The knife flashed as he flicked it open. With great care, he carved his name into the wood, then handed the knife and paddle to Jimmy.

Jimmy added his name. So did Grin and Mush. The paddle got passed around. Every newsie who had ever caught it from Mr. Drinker added his name. Everyone except me.

When I got home, I stashed the paddle away. I felt so giddy that I picked up Ma and twirled her around. Ma wondered what had gotten into me and sniffed my breath. Maggie said to steer clear or she'd knock me out cold.

It just goes to show that if you do something foolish and fail, you're an idiot. If you succeed, you're a hero.

Saturday, June 10, 1899

Lots of fellas learn to swim in the East River, myself included. It's a dirty place to swim. You never know what will float by: rotten cabbages, apples, and bananas; broken wooden crates; swollen dead rats; and plenty of other garbage. We just push it aside and have fun.

This morning, Grin Boyle told Jimmy that there are two ways a fella can learn to swim. The first way is to toss him into the water from the pier. If the fella swims, that's good. If he sinks and screams for help, you laugh at him, then dive in and rescue him. I've seen plenty of fellas hauled to shallow water that way.

The second way goes like this: Tie rope around a fella's waist and then throw him off the pier. If he sinks, you reel him to the surface like a fish. Then you laugh at him and holler instructions, telling him to start kicking and paddling. Each time he sinks, you reel him back up and shout more directions.

Nervous! Never saw such a nervous fella as Jimmy! Jimmy is no coward — you can count on him in any fight — but he shook right down to his toes as he looked over the pier's edge. We explained to Jimmy that a husky fella like him would float better than most. But Jimmy said in a quavering voice that he did not want to be thrown off the pier, rope or no rope.

"Well, then, we'll have to think of another way to teach Jimmy," I said, and I brought out Mr. Drinker's paddle.

Jimmy's eyes bulged. Racetrack calmed him down and explained that the wooden paddle will help him float.

Jimmy needed proof, so we waded chest-deep into the river and took turns showing him how the paddle kept us afloat. Jimmy was amazed. Truth be told, the paddle didn't help us float — we were just pretending — but we wanted to encourage Jimmy, and he is pretty easy to sucker.

We showed Jimmy how to float on his back. Once Jimmy relaxed, he got the hang of it, and then we showed him how to float on his stomach. Pretty soon, with the paddle's help, Jimmy was kicking and paddling like a dog.

Confident now, Jimmy progressed quickly. By noon he was doggy-paddling around the pier. We climbed out and stretched out on our backs in the sun. Jimmy said, "I can't believe it. I can swim."

"That's right," said Racetrack. "It's time for your initiation."

Jimmy shrieked like a girl as Racetrack and I grabbed

his legs. Grin and Mush grabbed his arms. We rocked him and then heaved him off the pier. He hit the water like a sack of potatoes.

Jimmy popped to the surface, flailing his arms and screaming. Thinking he was drowning, I tossed him the paddle. But it wasn't the paddle he needed. His underwear popped up several feet away. He lunged for them, but they sailed downriver, carried away by the current. Jimmy was now swimming illegally.

That's when Jimmy discovered yet another use for Mr. Drinker's paddle. He used it to cover his front parts as he waded to shore.

Saturday, July 1, 1899

I am so tired that I can barely keep up my head to write these words. It has been three weeks since I have written in this journal. Each day spins past until it becomes a week.

For three weeks now, I've been rising before dawn. By seven o'clock I am hard at work, painting houses with Pop and Grandpa Jiggsy.

There's much work to painting a house, inside and out, but it's enough to make a fella die from boredom. Pop mixes the dry paint powder with the oil and turpentine.

Grandpa Jiggsy and I paint porch spindles and moldings while Pop and his painters climb up and down ladders to paint the house sides.

When I get home, I drag myself down to Newspaper Row to sell papers. The fellas are having fun without me, swimming in the East River, tormenting street peddlers, and sleeping out at Corlear's Hook Park. It makes my liver burn with envy.

Thursday, July 6, 1899

It was a steaming hot night, and we all woke up screaming and scratching. I leaped up from my bed, yanked off my nightshirt, and dug at my skin. In the next room, Annie and Winnie shrieked. Maggie screeched.

Ma and Pop leaped from bed. They carried the crying girls into the kitchen. Pop turned up the gaslight. We all stood in the kitchen, tearing and digging at our skin until it bled.

Annie and Winnie sat on the kitchen table, bawling, as Ma yanked off their nightclothes. They were covered in red bites. We were all covered in red bites and bedbugs. They crawled on our arms and legs and stomachs and backs. We slapped at them and scratched at them. They burst bright red from our blood.

Ma poured water and salt into a jar, mixed it up, and we all dabbed at our bites. The salt water burned.

Summer is the worst season for bedbugs. No matter how many times Ma douses the beds with kerosene and boils the sheets and bedding, the wingless bugs are everywhere.

To escape them, we scrambled to the rooftop to sleep. Other families were already there, heaped about, snoring and groaning and tossing and turning on mattresses and blankets and newspapers spread out for bedding. Quietly, Pop spread out leftover *Journals* for our bedding, and we settled ourselves on the newspapers.

I don't know what time it was when Grandpa Jiggsy found us on the roof. He peeled off his nightshirt and spread it out next to Pop, and then he lay down.

Suddenly Pop said, "Jiggsy, if you're sleeping *on* your nightshirt, what are you wearing?"

"My mustache," said Grandpa Jiggsy.

Pop got up and moved.

Sunday, July 9, 1899

After Mass, Pop rented a carriage and Ma packed a picnic lunch and we all rode out to Brooklyn to see the new houses that Pop and I have painted.

We stood on the unpaved streets as Pop pointed to the

row of tidy, freshly painted, two-story wooden houses, each an exact copy of its neighbor. The houses smelled of fresh paint and varnish and new wood. Real estate signs poked up between the weeds.

With pride, Pop pointed out all the work that we have done on each house. He told how we painted the clapboard siding, the cornices, the trim, and the small front porch and its spindles.

On tiptoes, Ma and Maggie peered into the windows. Pop described how we painted and varnished each room inside, from the crown moldings to the window trim. "Imagine this, Clare," said Pop. "Each house has six rooms and just one family. Each family has its own modern water closet with its own bathtub. No more waiting in line! Each kitchen has a cookstove and icebox! Electric lights! And someday, a telephone!"

"A telephone! Ma, did you hear that?" said Maggie.

"I heard," said Ma. "Those families are very fortunate."

Pop took Ma's hand and said, "We could be one of those families, Clare."

Ma said, "Johnny, we can't afford a house like this."

"Yes, we can," said Pop. "I have talked with Mr. Hoban about the terms. I give him a down payment. After that, I pay him ten dollars a week for ten years. In ten years, we own the house."

"That's forty dollars a month," said Ma. "That's more than double our rent."

"We can do it," said Pop. "Mr. Hoban likes my work, and he has pull with other builders. I will get more contracts." He swept his hand grandly at the skeletons of unfinished houses. "All these houses need to be painted. And there will be more."

"There's Finn's college," said Ma. "And a wedding for Maggie."

"We can do it," said Pop.

Ma turned her face from him and stared at the wooden houses. She was doing the arithmetic in her head as her eyes took in the narrow frames, the front porch, and the small weedy patch of yard. Ten dollars a week, fifty-two weeks each year, ten years. Plus a down payment.

She chewed her lip. I knew she was thinking how she doesn't like to buy on credit, how she doesn't like to be beholden to people. But Pop had contracts to paint ten more houses, and he would get more. Pop was his own boss at last. And this was a tomorrow house. Not a someday house. I could see the wishing in Ma's eyes. Was it too good to be true?

"What do you think, Clare?" said Pop.

"I think that you, Johnny Reardon, are a man of considerable talent," said Ma.

Pop threw his hat in the air and picked up Ma and kissed her and spun her around until her shoes flew off.

Monday, July 10, 1899

Pop was touchy all day. This morning, he complained that Palo used too much paint and Alberto painted too slowly. Then he said that Grandpa Jiggsy goes to the toilet too often and takes too long. He called them all loafers.

By noon, Pop had decided that Carlo was the worst loafer of all because he was sick and kept throwing up. He found Carlo sitting, looking green in the face, and Pop fired him right on the spot. "You should have seen how fast the others worked after that," Pop told Ma. "No more loafing."

Ma asked if Carlo had a family. Pop didn't know.

Wednesday, July 12, 1899

Pop has been touchier than usual. We are nearly done with the last house, and today he fired Mariano, who suffers from the same stomach sickness as Carlo. Mariano also complained that he saw spots before his eyes.

My father has become an expert in these matters. He says there are two times to fire a worker: at the beginning of a job, to show the other workers you mean business, and at the end of a job, to show them you still mean business.

Thursday, July 13, 1899

Tonight Pop stumbled home and collapsed onto a kitchen chair. "Quick! Get me a bucket!" he groaned to Ma.

She brought one and he threw up. "I have been sick all day," he said.

Ma touched his cheek. "You don't have a fever," she said. She opened the airshaft window and told him to stick his head outside and breathe the air.

He did and then he threw up down the airshaft.

"You're working too hard," said Ma. "You need to hire more painters."

"If I hire more, then I must pay more," said Pop.

"It's better to pay than to be sick like this," said Ma.

"My head hurts," said Pop. "I hurt all over." He blinked and rubbed his eyes. "I see spots," he said. Ma gave him a cold towel to cover his eyes and we helped him to bed. Pop threw up again, and now he is lying in bed, groaning.

Friday, July 14, 1899

I am sitting on my stoop, watching Annie and Winnie while Ma sits at the doctor's office. I am waiting for news about Pop. This morning, Pop had a dizzy spell and he fell from the ladder. Two stories.

I didn't see it happen. All I know is that Pop mixed the paint, and then he climbed the ladder propped against the gable end of the house. A few minutes later, I heard a shout and then a sickening thud. Pop was lying on the ground, moaning, his arm and leg bent at queer angles. I ran to hire a wagon. Grandpa Jiggsy, Palo, and Alberto lifted Pop onto a board and into the wagon. We got him to the Bowery doctor and then I went to tell Ma.

Now there's nothing to do but sit and scribble here while I wait for news. Near me, a group of girls are huddled over their jacks and rubber balls. They are talking girl-talk, and their words and giggles drift over to me, telling me more than I want to know.

Later

Pop is home, propped up in bed, his arm and leg wrapped in thick plaster casting. His moans fill the flat.

The doctor said Pop is a lucky man because he only broke his arm and leg. Though it will take a good eight weeks for the bones to mend, the doctor said Pop is luckier than many painters. Many fallen painters have broken their necks or backs. Some have even died.

The doctor told us about painter's sickness. When the oil and turpentine are mixed with the dry paint powder, it creates fumes that make the painters dizzy and sick to their stomachs. It becomes a poison that affects the nervous system. It has something to do with the lead in the paint powder.

Pop looks small and thin lying on the bed. He called to me and I went in to see him. He pulled me close and said, "Promise me that you will stay in school. Promise me that you will make something out of yourself so that you never have to suffer like your father."

I didn't know what to say. Promise that I will stay in school? That's like asking an inmate to stay in jail.

Saturday, July 15, 1899

Last night it was hot out, and I was far away in my head as I waited to buy my *Journals*. I was thinking about Pop, lying in bed with his arm and leg in plaster casting.

Mr. Needle yelled, "Next," and snapped me back to Newspaper Row. I pushed sixty cents over the counter and said one hundred papers.

I grabbed my bundle and headed to my corner. I guess I was thinking too much about Pop and not enough about selling papers because later when I counted my money, I came up five cents short. I counted the money three times, but each time the same five cents was missing. Did I give out too much change?

Sunday, July 16, 1899

Pop sleeps hard, as though he's dead. We get him awake enough to spoon some soup into him, but then he falls right back to sleep. One time he cried out, "Too much paint!" and waved his good arm as though he was shaking his fist.

There's a part of me that feels like shaking my fist at Pop. I remember once how Grandpa Jiggsy said a boss has to look out for his workers and how Grandpa Jiggsy looked out for his snow shovelers. Well, Pop didn't look out for his workers. He didn't even look out for himself.

Later

Tonight, Ma sat Maggie and me down and we discussed our finances. Grandpa Jiggsy will finish painting the last house, but after that, there are no more contracts. Mr. Hoban has found somebody else to paint his houses.

For two months, Ma said, we will receive the sick benefit from the Irish Brotherhood Benevolent Association. That money and our savings will help us pay our bills: the wages Pop owes his workers; the painting supplies he bought on credit; and the doctor, groceries, and rent.

I looked at the morning glory plate and then at Ma. "Our savings is your house money," I said. "That's not fair!"

"So be it," said Ma. "Life isn't always fair."

Pop groaned from the bedroom. She got up and took the slop bucket to him.

Monday, July 17, 1899

I have never felt so low-down. Tonight I bought one hundred *Journals*, determined to stay out till midnight to sell them all for Ma.

I needed to sell sixty to break even, and I had sold forty-five when it started to rain. After that, I sold only three more papers. When I counted my money, I should have had forty-eight cents and a nickel in tips, making fifty-three cents. Somehow I came up short eight cents.

Now I am kicking myself. It was stupid and foolish to buy one hundred papers on a Monday night with no good headlines and a chance of rain. I lost fifteen cents and have enough leftover *Journals* to cut into wipes for the rest of July.

Tuesday, July 18, 1899

It turns out I wasn't the only newsie short last night. So were Racetrack, Jimmy, Grin, and Mush. Racetrack says Mr. Needle is choking us down, so tonight Racetrack counted his papers at Mr. Needle's window. "Hey," he said. "You shorted me five papers!"

"They were all there when I gave them to you, kid," said Mr. Needle. "Now hit the road."

Racetrack glowered at Mr. Needle. "You're shorting us papers," he said in an even voice. "We ain't going to stand for it. You wait and see."

"The only thing I want to see is the back of your head," said Mr. Needle. "Now get out before I call the cops."

Racetrack grabbed his papers and headed down News-paper Row, telling every *Journal* newsie to meet tomorrow in City Hall Park. He said it's time we stand up for our rights.

Wednesday, July 19, 1899

This afternoon, *Journal* newsies filled City Hall Park. I had brought Mr. Drinker's paddle along and held it up as a signal to begin our meeting. The newsies fell quiet.

Racetrack stood in front of the newsies. "All we want is fair play," he said. "It's time for Hearst and Pulitzer to play fair with us."

The newsies whistled and clapped and cheered, and I could feel myself being swept away with excitement.

Racetrack punctuated the word "time" by punching at the air. "It's *time* for those rich gents to roll back the cost we pay for our papers. It's *time* we tell them that we'll pay fifty cents for one hundred papers and not one cent more." Fist raised, he shouted, "Or else it's *time* that we strike!"

All through City Hall Park, newsies picked up the chant: "Strike! Strike! Strike!"

I raised the paddle again. The chanting stopped. A fella named Morris Cohen spoke next. He said we should elect officers and plan our strike strategy.

Jimmy nominated Racetrack. Everybody knows Racetrack, and fellas shouted approval. Then Grin nominated me. "Finn who?" someone shouted. "The fella who stole the paddle!" Grin shouted back.

Racetrack and I won easily. So did several older fellas: Kid Blink, Barney Peters, Crutchy Morris, Abe Newman, and Dave Simons.

Kid Blink spoke next. He broke into a confident grin and told us that he was sending Hearst and Pulitzer a message: Our union would give them twenty-four hours to roll back the wholesale price of their newspapers. If they refused, we would strike.

Next Kid Blink told us we needed a committee on discipline. He appointed a small, tough-looking fella as leader. The boy stood and said, "We can do in any scab newsboy that shows his face. We're here for our rights and we'll die defending them." The newsies clapped and howled.

Kid Blink picked delegates to spread word of the strike to the newsies at Fifty-ninth Street and in Harlem, Brooklyn, Long Island, and Jersey.

The meeting was adjourned. Racetrack laughed to himself as we headed home, in a kind of happy disbelief. He took the paddle from me. "What do you suppose Mr. Drinker would say if he knew this was our emblem?" he asked.

Mimicking Mr. Drinker I said, "Mr. Higgins, I believe you have a certain item of mine."

Racetrack laughed. "This was a great night," he said, handing back the paddle. Then he said we'll win in a walk if we stick together.

Now I am home, and the paddle is safely hidden behind the sofa. I am sitting at the kitchen table, turning over the day's events in my head. It *was* a great night. It feels good to be a strike leader.

Thursday, July 20, 1899

This morning I got up, sure that Mr. Hearst and Mr. Pulitzer would come to their senses. But I soon realized they do not want their newsies to tell them how to run their newspaper business.

Tonight Racetrack slid two bits toward Mr. Needle and said, "One hundred papers."

Mr. Needle glanced at the fifty cents and then said, "What are you trying to pull, kid? You know one hundred papers cost sixty cents."

Racetrack looked him in the eye and said, "Perhaps you haven't heard. We told Hearst that we ain't paying more than fifty cents."

Mr. Needle pushed the money back and snapped, "Then you aren't getting your papers. Next!"

Racetrack turned and shouted to us, "Did you hear that? Hearst still wants his ten cents. What do you fellas say?"

"Strike!" they shouted back. "Strike! Strike! Strike!"

As the chanting filled the street, we heard the familiar rattle of *Journal* delivery wagons heading out of the alley. The wagons were loaded with newspapers for the uptown, Harlem, Brooklyn, Long Island, and Jersey City newsies.

"Stop the scabs!" yelled Kid Blink.

Newsies filled the street and charged. Outnumbered, the drivers jumped and fled down Park Row. We toppled the abandoned wagons and swarmed over the spilled newspapers, grabbing them and tearing them. The streets began to look as though the sky were snowing newspapers.

Racetrack grabbed a bundle. "Nobody's selling these scab sheets," he said, ripping them to shreds.

Jimmy and Grin joined in. Mush tossed me a bundle and turned to grab another.

At that moment, Mr. Needle rushed out of his office, shaking his fist and hollering at us. From somewhere, a tomato sailed at him and splattered against his shirt.

He turned and ran back into his office. He bolted the door and shuttered the windows. Police whistles shrilled. "Cheese it!" Kid Blink yelled. "It's the cops."

Everyone scattered. Still clutching the newspapers, I ran and didn't stop running until I reached Division Street. My legs shaking, I realized that I was still holding the newspaper bundle. One hundred newspapers in all.

I knew I should rip up the scab sheets and throw them away, but I felt all stirred up, thinking how I had one hundred papers at pure profit. A whole dollar in sales, not counting tips, could go in my pocket. I thought about Ma and how much we needed the money, with Pop laid up and out of work.

But I knew it wouldn't feel good, handing that money over to Ma. And I knew how disappointed she would be, if she knew how I earned it. Ma expected me to stick up for my rights. And to finish my fights.

Just then a gent hurried toward me. "Hey, kid, are you selling the *Journal*?" he asked, holding out a nickel.

"These *Journals* aren't for sale," I told him. "In case you haven't heard, the newsies are on strike." Then I handed him a newspaper and told him to keep his money.

It hurt giving all those newspapers away, but newsies have to stick together. If we don't stick together, it's not a union. It's dog-eat-dog.

Friday, July 21, 1899

Something Mr. Watkins told me keeps ticking in my head. He said that words bring about change. There's got to be a way I can use words to bring about change.

Saturday, July 22, 1899

This morning one hundred newsies waited for Mr. Hearst outside the *Journal* office building. Soon a shiny black automobile came down the street. Someone shouted, "Here he comes!" The automobile pulled up to the curb, and a man wearing a fancy hat and coat stepped out.

"Mr. Hearst!" yelled a newsie.

"Pipe down," said another. "That's the driver."

The driver opened the back door, and a tall, long-legged gent emerged from the backseat. It was Mr. Hearst, wearing a checked suit, a hard-brimmed straw hat, and a bunched ascot tie under his chin.

"Mr. Hearst!" yelled Racetrack. "We're the strikers!"

Hearing that, Mr. Hearst paused. "Well, boys, what can I do for you?" he said in a high, soft voice. He had a long face with close-set eyes and a strained smile.

Racetrack stepped forward. "We want one hundred papers for fifty cents, not sixty," he said. "The difference is only a dime."

Mr. Hearst told us that he cannot afford to sell papers to us for less. He said it takes a great deal of money to publish a newspaper, more money than we could ever imagine. He said he spent $100,000 last year on foreign correspondents sent to cover the Spanish-American War and he has to recover his costs.

"Do you have any idea how many dimes it takes to make up a loss like that?" said Mr. Hearst.

"One million," Racetrack told him, just like that.

That surprised Mr. Hearst. He chuckled and told Racetrack that he had a good head for numbers. Then he eyed us all, as though he was sizing us up, and said, "Why don't a few of you boys come in and we'll talk it over?"

Kid Blink, Dave Simons, and Racetrack followed Mr. Hearst into the building.

When they came out, Kid Blink announced that Mr. Hearst would give us an answer on Monday. In the meantime, Kid Blink said, we should pursue our strike relentlessly to show the *Journal* and the *World* that we mean business.

The newsies scattered to look for scabs, but I cut across City Hall Park and headed for Murphy's Saloon. I pushed open the heavy doors. It felt like a cool, dark cave inside, filled with smoke. My eyes adjusted to the dim light, and I spotted a familiar brown fedora on a gent seated at the bar. It was Mr. Watkins, scribbling away in his notebook.

I went up to him and asked if he remembered me. He said, "Of course. You're Finn Reardon, the newsie with an eye for detail." He asked if I had a scoop for him. I told him yes, as a matter of a fact, I did. I told him that the *Journal* and the *World* newsies were on strike.

Mr. Watkins grinned and said he knew about the newsboys' strike. He said it was about time that David stood up to Goliath.

I always liked that Bible story about young David and how he felled the giant Goliath with a simple slingshot. I reminded Mr. Watkins what he told me, about the power of words and how they bring about change. Then I said, "Mr. Watkins, maybe you can help the newsies by writing about the strike."

Mr. Watkins thought it over. Then he shook his head and said, "I'm sorry, Finn, but I'm not the best reporter for the job."

My heart turned over, hearing that. "I don't know anyone else who can cover the strike," I said.

"Yes, you do," he said.

"Who?" I said.

He gripped my shoulder and pointed behind the bar. I

looked past the bartender polishing the bar with a white towel, past the rows of bottles, and into the long mirror. I blinked. Mr. Watkins was pointing at me.

Sunday, July 23, 1899

At last, I'm not just the fella who shouts the headlines on the street. I am the fella who makes the news! Mr. Watkins and I have an agreement: I will gather information about the strike and he will write the article.

Mr. Watkins says we will sell a good many articles to newspapers like the *Sun*, the *Herald*, and the *Times*, who don't feel the least bit sorry for Mr. Hearst and Mr. Pulitzer. The rival newspapers will be happy to publish as many articles as they can.

A freelance reporter gets paid space-rates, which means the more information I gather, the more Mr. Watkins can write, and the more money we will both make.

I promised Mr. Watkins that I will be a reporter he can trust.

Monday, July 24, 1899

Today while the newsies were waiting for Mr. Hearst's answer, we found out that he and Mr. Pulitzer do not intend to negotiate. They sent agents to all the bars and flophouses along the Bowery, looking for men to sell the scab sheets. They offered the men two dollars a day. That's more money than some newsies make in a week!

Tonight I am covering a mass meeting of newsies at Irving Hall on Broome Street.

Tuesday, July 25, 1899

Last night Irving Hall was crowded with two thousand newsies from uptown, downtown, Brooklyn, Hoboken, and Jersey City. Three thousand more waited outside.

The meeting lasted two hours. Dave Simons appealed to the public, asking them to help us win our fight by boycotting the *Journal* and the *World*. To the newsies, he said, "We're going to win this fight, boys — only we must stick together and hold firm."

Then Kid Blink got up and told us to stick together like glue. Then he said what the newsies have been saying all along: Ten cents on a hundred papers means more to a newsboy than it does to a millionaire. Irving Hall filled with cheers and whistles.

Then Kid Blink asked the newsies to let up on the scabs and drivers. "No more violence," he said. "Let's win the strike on the square." That struck me odd, since Kid Blink and Dave were right up front, leading the charge, when the newsies toppled the wagons and tore up the scab newspapers.

Then Kid Blink and Dave Simons promised us all a monster parade with three bands: one for the Manhattan boys, one for the Brooklyn boys, and one for the Harlem boys. The meeting ended, and five thousand newsies howled like demons and ran out of the hall.

Mr. Watkins told me I did a good job capturing all the quotes.

Thursday, July 27, 1899

No monster parade. Kid Blink said that the city denied us a parade permit. When Kid Blink talks now, there's something about him that doesn't seem right to me. I don't know what it is for sure, but I get a feeling about him that I don't trust.

Friday, July 28, 1899

The *Journal* and the *World* advertised again for men to sell the newspapers. This time they offered two dollars a day plus forty cents for every one hundred newspapers sold. Seven hundred men signed up. To our dismay, we spotted Dave Simons and some other fellas coming down Frankfort Street. They each carried bundles of scab sheets to sell.

Someone yelled, "Traitor!" Newsies mobbed Dave and his friends, ripping and tearing the newspapers. The police came to break up the riot.

At that moment, someone spotted Kid Blink, also carrying newspapers. He was wearing new clothes.

"He's been bought off," said Racetrack. It felt like a sucker punch as we realized that Racetrack was right.

"Traitor!" Mush yelled.

Hearing that, Kid Blink threw down his papers and ran. A hundred newsies chased him up Park Row. More cops came running, blowing their whistles and swinging their nightsticks.

Kid Blink turned the corner onto Frankfort Street and ran into two detectives. Lucky for Kid Blink, the cops arrested him on the spot and charged him — wrongly — with leading a mob.

Saturday, July 29, 1899

Not one copy of a scab sheet can be found in any district. In Brooklyn, newsies tip over *Journal* and *World* delivery wagons and tear up the sheets. When the delivery wagons pull up to the ferries, the Jersey City newsies swoop down and capture the papers as they are thrown down at the loading docks. The Yonkers boys lie in wait for the trains, and then they sweep down and capture the papers as they arrive.

How much longer can Mr. Hearst and Mr. Pulitzer hold out?

Wednesday, August 2, 1899

The strike is over. Although nothing official has been said, we got word that Mr. Hearst and Mr. Pulitzer have agreed to a compromise: The wholesale price of the *Journal* and the *World* will remain the same, but they have agreed to take back all unsold papers, one hundred percent.

Friday, August 4, 1899

Mr. Watkins and I made quite a team. He earned so much money selling freelance articles to the *Sun* that the city news editor offered him a full-time reporter's job. Mr. Watkins treated me to a fifteen-cent beef-and-beans dinner at Hitchcock's in the Tribune Building, where a fella can eat as much bread as he wants without asking. After dinner, Mr. Watkins told me that I could visit him at the *Sun*'s city newsroom anytime. I told him to look for me on August 18, the day I turn fourteen.

Friday, August 25, 1899

The past few weeks have felt like I dropped a newspaper on a street corner and the wind is coming off the East River, blowing the sheets away faster than I can run and catch them.

Last Friday was my birthday. I went to see Mr. Watkins at the *Sun* office. I climbed the spiral iron staircase that winds its way through a gloomy shaft to the city newsroom on the third floor. The walls trembled and echoed with the rumble of the printing presses in the cellar.

The city newsroom was just as I had imagined: a madhouse! Reporters were bent over inclined desks, writing the news that newsies would shout. Copyboys carrying articles from desk to desk. One editor shouting orders. Another arguing with a reporter over commas. A pressman arguing with a man over headline type size.

When Mr. Watkins spotted me, he practically leaped over his desk to shake my hand. He introduced me all around, telling the reporters about my eye for detail. I was glad to hear that. I was worried that Mr. Watkins may have gotten too big to remember me, now that he's a full-time reporter.

Finally, we got some time to talk privately. He asked about Pop and I told him that Pop is up and about, still in casts, but hobbling around our flat on crutches. His stomach and nerves are bad from the painter's sickness, and the doctor told him that he must not paint anymore. Ma told Pop that he is a man of considerable talent and there are plenty of jobs he can do, but now that Pop has been a boss, he doesn't want to be anything less.

I told Mr. Watkins that I know how Pop feels. I used to feel that my journal kept me going. But lately, I can't bear the thought of writing in it. Maybe it's because I got a taste of what it's like to be a reporter, no matter what.

I told Mr. Watkins I'm fourteen now and want to work at a newspaper like the *Sun*. I told him that I'm willing to do anything it takes to become a reporter, no matter what.

Mr. Watkins thought about that. Then he said, "You'll do anything it takes? No matter how hard?"

"I'm not afraid of hard work," I told him.

"Good," he said. "Then stay in school. That's what it takes to be a reporter."

School, my arse, I wanted to say. But I didn't.

Monday, September 11, 1899

School is jail for children, but it lets its prisoners out at three. There's not much I want to say about school except that our jailer is a tall, slim, bony, faultfinding man named Mr. Drinker who has been promoted to the seventh grade. He starts each day the same way. Miserably. There's one difference: He no longer has a paddle hanging on the back of his closet door.

Epilogue

Even though it meant suffering through another year of Mr. Drinker, Finn Reardon did what it took to become a reporter: He stayed in school. Jimmy Vaskey and Thomas "Racetrack" Higgins quit school after sixth grade. Grin Boyle and Mush Myers completed the eighth grade. But the "fellas" remained loyal friends for the rest of their lives. At his high school graduation, Finn presented Mr. Drinker with his wooden paddle.

Finn won a scholarship to Columbia University, where he studied history and literature. While in college, he worked as a copyboy at the New York *Sun*. After college, Finn became a reporter for the *Sun*. He remained interested in labor issues, and he covered the 1909–1910 garment workers' strikes in New York City and the 1911 Triangle Shirtwaist Fire. He traveled throughout the United States, reporting on unfair labor practices and conditions.

When World War I broke out in 1914, Finn went to

Europe, where he worked for the Red Cross as an ambulance litter bearer. In his journal, he detailed his experiences and the horrors of war: the chemical gases, the trenches, and the tanks.

In 1917, the United States entered the war. Mush Myers, Grin Boyle, and Jimmy Vaskey enlisted right away. Mush Myers was wounded in the leg by a mortar shell at the Austrian front. He was taken to an emergency canteen at Fossalta, where he met — and later married — a Red Cross nurse.

Jimmy Vaskey fought bravely in the Battle of Meuse-Argonne. After the war, Jimmy married and worked as a newspaper dealer. He owned and operated a newsstand on Fifth Avenue. Grin Boyle worked at the cigarette factory for the rest of his life.

Racetrack Higgins never married. He owned and operated a speakeasy during Prohibition. In 1928, he died trying to make peace between two men who were arguing over a gambling debt.

When Finn returned home from World War I, he continued to write. Though he remained shy around girls, he often wrote and sold romantic short stories to serials like *Collier's* and the *Saturday Evening Post*. After graduation, Finn never saw Bootsie Weber again, but many of his short stories featured a redheaded girl as their heroine.

In 1920, Finn met Alma Carrigan in the reading room

at the New York Public Library. They married two months later. He considered it fortuitous that Alma had red hair and eyes the color of morning glories. They had two daughters.

Finn's father died in 1922, and his mother died the following year. In 1926, Finn wrote a successful novel based on his war experiences. He and Alma bought a small white house in Brooklyn. They planted morning glories all around its white picket fence.

Life in America
in 1899

Historical Note

Finn Reardon, his family and friends, and other characters in this book are works of fiction, but the newsboy strike of 1899 really happened. Actual newsies named Racetrack Higgins, Grin Boyle, Mush Myers, Kid Blink, and Dave Simons participated in the newsboys' strike.

At the turn of the twentieth century, New York City was experiencing growing pains. In slightly more than nine years' time, its population had doubled, rising from 1.5 million in 1890 to 3 million in 1899.

In 1899, the Bowery district was one of the most densely populated areas in New York City's Lower East Side. The district extended six blocks on both sides of the infamous mile-long Bowery street, an area well known for its pawnshops, saloons, missions, cheap lodging houses, high crime rate, and crowded, unsanitary tenements.

Children walked to city schools in groups for protection from neighborhood gangs. The school curricula consisted of citizenship, morals and manners, and basic education in reading, writing, American history, geography, spelling, and arithmetic. Students memorized lessons and recited them, word for word, to the teacher while standing at attention. Teachers maintained strict discipline, often using a wooden paddle or ruler.

Parents tried to keep their children in school as long as possible — at least long enough to finish grammar school, or the sixth grade. But that wasn't always possible, especially when they needed money to help put groceries on the table and to pay rent, doctor's bills, and other necessities. By age fourteen, many tenement children quit school to work full-time. Many younger children worked illegally.

More boys than girls worked in the street trades. Parents were protective of their daughters and often restricted them to unpaid work at home. Girls worked alongside their mothers, cooking, cleaning, running errands, doing the daily shopping, and helping with laundry. They minded younger brothers and sisters. When mothers took in industrial homework — finishing work or sewing — the daughters helped.

City streets provided ample opportunity for boys to make money outside the home. An enterprising boy could scavenge for glass, paper, rags, and other discarded items to sell to the junkman. He could shine shoes, run errands, deliver messages, and sell anything from gum to candy to newspapers.

Selling newspapers was the most popular work for city boys. Contrary to popular representation, most newsboys were not orphans, homeless street waifs, or the sole support of a widowed mother and siblings. Most newsboys slept and ate at home. They sold newspapers after school and on weekends. Unlike children who worked in factories and sweatshops, newsboys tended to like their jobs because they enjoyed the freedom and excitement of the street.

New York City's population explosion brought forth a whole new class of newspaper customers: the working class, comprised of the middle and lower classes. When publisher Joseph Pulitzer realized that the huge masses of working-class people had no newspaper to speak for them, he saw a need and a customer. He had a simple but innovative newspaper philosophy: to appeal to the reader's mind, emotions, and heartstrings and to provide the news first and give more of it. He expected his reporters to look for news, rather than wait for news. The formula worked. When Pulitzer bought the New York *World* in 1883, it had a circulation of 22,761. By 1895, its daily circulation had increased to 370,000. (The next largest newspapers, the New York *Herald* and the *Sun*, each sold 120,000.)

In 1895, publisher William Randolph Hearst purchased the New York *Journal*. Like Pulitzer, Hearst wanted to create a best-selling newspaper. But, whereas

Pulitzer used forward-thinking and innovative techniques, Hearst simply copied Pulitzer's successful formula. The *Journal* imitated the *World*'s design, page and column size, and type. Like Pulitzer, Hearst realized that the growing numbers of working-class people presented a huge market. But Hearst's philosophy differed from Pulitzer's in this way: Hearst wanted to give readers a daily dose of lurid stories, juicy scandals, and shocking news. He believed these stories would ultimately sell the most newspapers.

Hearst lured reporters away from Pulitzer with generous contracts. He also lured away Pulitzer's most popular comic-strip artist, Richard Outcault, the creator of a comic strip called "Hogan's Alley," which featured a gap-toothed kid who had big ears and funny toes and who wore bright yellow clothes. When Outcault left Pulitzer to work for Hearst, the comic strip still belonged legally to the *World*. To get around this, Outcault simply named his new comic strip "The Yellow Kid." This outraged Pulitzer, and the two publishers fought over the right to "The Yellow Kid." Rival newspapers watched gleefully. When one editor referred to the battle as "yellow journalism," the apt term stuck. Today, "yellow journalism" refers to newspapers that sensationalize and distort the news.

Through the mid-1890s, the *Journal*'s daily circulation

grew until it matched the *World*'s — about 430,000 daily. During this time, tension increased between the United States and Spain.

For many years, Cubans had been trying unsuccessfully to free themselves from Spanish rule. As stories about the cruel treatment of Cubans by Spanish soldiers circulated throughout the United States, many Americans grew angry. They sympathized with the Cubans.

The *Journal* and the *World* began a propaganda campaign and sent reporters to Cuba. Though the sufferings of the Cuban people were real, the reporters wrote exaggerated accounts. The two publishers competed with each other in extra editions and splashy headlines.

Two events brought matters to a head: On February 8, 1898, the *Journal* published a letter written by the Spanish minister to the United States. In the letter, the Spanish minister criticized President McKinley, calling him weak. This infuriated many Americans. One week later, a mysterious explosion sank the U.S.S. *Maine* in Havana harbor, killing 259 officers and men. Although no cause for the explosion has ever been determined, the yellow newspapers accused the Spanish. On April 25, 1898, the United States declared war against Spain.

With the declaration, newspaper circulation soared. During the first week, the *World* boasted that it sold 5 million newspapers. When the war ended three months later, the two publishers were each selling 1.3 million daily copies.

But Pulitzer and Hearst had also spent a great deal of money competing with each other in news coverage, extra editions, splashy front pages, and foreign correspondents. They spent more than they could hope to recoup in advertising and sales. To recover their losses, they raised the wholesale cost of the newspapers from fifty cents to sixty cents for one hundred papers.

During the war, the newsboys sold papers at fever pitch. As long as the newsboys were making money hawking extra editions, they did not protest the price increase. When the war ended, the newspaper sales declined and so did the boys' profits.

Though it's difficult to say where or exactly how the newsboys' strike began, the first reported action took place on July 18, 1899, when the Long Island City newsies discovered that they had been shorted papers. They attacked the deliveryman: They tipped over his wagon and chased him out of town.

From there, the strike grew. The boys organized and demanded that Joseph Pulitzer and William Randolph Hearst roll back the wholesale price of their newspapers. When the publishers refused, the newsboys went out on strike. The strike lasted two weeks and ended in a compromise, as described in Finn's journal.

As they get ready to sell their papers, newsies pose for a picture.

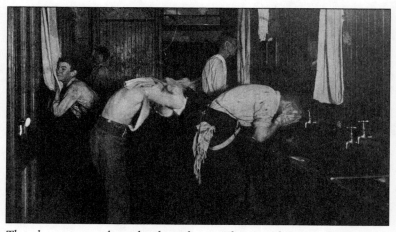

Though most newsboys lived at home, The Newsboys' Lodging House on Duane Street, near Newspaper Row, provided breakfast, supper, a bed, and night school to runaways. It was one of five houses run by the Children's Aid Society in New York City.

This view of City Hall Park offers a look at Newspaper Row, where the newsboys gathered each day. The large domed building is Joseph Pulitzer's World.

Young newsboys buy their newspapers from the circulation manager.

Joseph Pulitzer, publisher of the New York World, *created his newspaper for the middle and lower classes. Today he is known for endowments of monetary prizes and scholarships for distinction in journalism, letters, and music.*

William Randolph Hearst, publisher of the New York Journal, *created a vast chain of popular newspapers, based on sensational reporting, banner headlines, and low prices.*

150

Two children bring home "finishing work," or sewing to be done at home.

Children pose in an alleyway between tenement houses in the Lower East Side.

Author Note

When asked about *The Journal of Finn Reardon, a Newsie*, Susan Campbell Bartoletti said, "I wanted to tell Finn Reardon's story because it reveals a unique perspective on city kids who lived and worked over one hundred years ago.

"By 1900, nearly one million children worked in mills, in mines, in factories, in homes and fields, and on city streets selling newspapers and other items, delivering messages, and blacking boots. Most working children were ages seven to sixteen. From today's perspective, we can see that these kids were horribly exploited and victimized, but we can also see that some children — especially those who sold newspapers — enjoyed their work. They were empowered by their wages and by the independent nature of their work. Best of all, we can see that kids acted like kids whenever they could get away with it.

"I was particularly drawn to the story of the 1899 newsboys' strike because it shows the spirit, courage, and strength of children who banded together for a common cause. I taught eighth grade for eighteen years, and from that experience, I know that kids today also have a strong sense of justice and fair play. I admire their courage and spirit.

"As for Mr. Drinker's paddle? Suffice it to say that my sixth-grade teacher had a wooden paddle. I'll never forget the day he paddled two boys who didn't do their homework. I was so affected that my best friend and I plotted to steal his paddle so that he could never use it again. We never did, but I am very glad that Finn Reardon did."

Susan Campbell Bartoletti is an award-winning author of fiction and nonfiction for young people. Her many books include nonfiction titles such as *Black Potatoes: The Story of the Great Irish Famine*, winner of the ALA Sibert Award, NCTE Orbis Pictus Award, and the SCBWI Golden Kite for distinguished nonfiction; and *Kids on Strike!*, an ALA Best Book for Young Adults; novels such as *A Coal Miner's Bride* (in the Dear America line) and *No Man's Land: A Young Soldier's Story*; and picture books such as *The Christmas Promise*, illustrated by David Christiana. During the summer, she teaches creative writing in the Graduate Program of Children's Literature at Hollins University, Roanoke, Virginia. During the rest of the year she lives in Pennsylvania with her husband and family.

This book is dedicated to the Hollins Boot Campers: Lisa Rowe Fraustino, Han Nolan, and Ann Sullivan.

Acknowledgments

Some day-to-day events leading to the strike are products of imagination; others have been reconstructed through research of contemporary newspapers, magazines, books, maps, oral histories, biographies, and photographs, as well as books and articles published on the subject in recent years.

I am grateful to the following people: editor Beth Levine for her patience, gentle insistence, and belief in Finn; Betsy Partridge and Laurie Halse Anderson for their long-distance sisterhood; my writers group; Thom Brucie for sharing pages; and my husband, Joe, and my kids, Brandy, Joey, and now Rick, for helping me keep things in perspective.

Grateful acknowledgment is made for permission to reprint the following:

Cover Portrait: Brown Brothers.

Cover Background: Hester Street near Essex, Lower East Side, 1899. Courtesy of the Museum of the City of New York.

Page 148   (top): Newsies, Photography collections of the University of Maryland, Baltimore County.
Page 148   (bottom): The Newsboys' Lodging House, Library of Congress, Photograph by Jacob A. Riis.
Page 149   (top): View of Newspaper Row, Library of Congress.
Page 149   (bottom): Newsies buying their papers, Photography collections of the University of Maryland, Baltimore County.
Page 150   (top): Joseph Pulitzer, Library of Congress.
Page 150   (bottom): William Randolph Hearst, Bettman/ CORBIS.
Page 151   (top): Children bringing home "finishing work," Photography collections of the University of Maryland, Baltimore County.
Page 151   (bottom): Children posing an in alley, Museum of the City of New York, Photograph by Jacob A. Riis.

Other Dear America books About New York City

Dreams in the Golden Country
The Diary of Zipporah Feldman, a Jewish Immigrant Girl
by Kathryn Lasky

One Eye Laughing, The Other Weeping
The Diary of Julie Weiss
by Barry Denenberg

When Christmas Comes Again
The World War I Diary of Simone Spencer
by Beth Seidel Levine

Other Dear America books by Susan Cambell Bartoletti

A Coal Miner's Bride
The Diary of Anetka Kaminska

While the events described and some of the characters in this book may be based on actual historical events and real people, Finn Reardon is a fictional character, created by the author, and his journal and its epilogue are works of fiction.

Library of Congress Cataloging-in-Publication Data

Bartoletti, Susan Campbell.
The journal of Finn Reardon, newsie / by Susan Campbell Bartoletti.
p. cm. — (My Name Is America)
Summary: Finn Reardon, a thirteen-year-old Irish-American newspaper
carrier who hopes to be a journalist someday, keeps a journal of his experi-
ences living in New York City in 1899. Includes historical notes.
ISBN 0-439-18894-6
[1. Irish Americans — Juvenile Fiction.   2. Irish Americans — Fiction.
3. Newspaper carriers — Fiction.   4. Diaries — Fiction.   5. New York
(N.Y.) — History — 1898–1951 — Juvenile Fiction.   6. New York (N.Y.) —
History — 1898–1951 — Fiction.]   I. Title.   II. Series.
PZ7.B2844 Jo 2003
[Fic] — 21   2002030874
CIP AC

10   9   8   7   6   5   4   3   2   1   03   04   05   06   07

The display type was set in Bodoni Poster.
The text type was set in Berling Roman.
Book design by Elizabeth B. Parisi
Photo research by Sharon Lennon and Amla Sanghvi

Printed in the U.S.A.   23
First edition, May 2003

❖